NO WORDS BETWEEN US

CHRISTIE WALKER BOS

flying trees publishing

Published by
Flying Trees Publishing
www.flyingtreespublishing.com
First Edition

Cover design by Robbie Bos.

The characters, events, and places portrayed in this book are fictitious, *except for Rae*. Any similarity to real persons, living or dead, is coincidental and not intended by the author.

Library of Congress Control Number: 2023936234

ISBN: 978-1-955552-09-7 (e-book)
ISBN: 978-1-955552-10-3 (paperback)
ISBN: 978-1-955552-11-0 (hardcover)

DEDICATION

For our dogs, and the people who love them.

The Community Garden - 4.6 stars on Amazon

A Creative and Fun Read "A creative and fun "who done it" with believable characters. I loved reading the witty and entertaining narrative and did not expect the ending. Highly recommended!"

A Mystery Worth Dying For "A mystery that makes you want to hunt down the killer, and leaves you surprised, only be left with a cheer and a tear in the end."

What a Delightful Read "Walker Bos' characters are believable and come to life with a slow reveal. Although not all characters are "good," there are no real villains to root against. The organization builds suspense and makes the story flow easily to a beautiful and sympathetic conclusion."

Fearless - 4.8 stars on Amazon

Funny, Moving, Heartfelt "This book is such a great story. It's realistic, with moments of joy, shock, sadness, and humor. Even before I finished it I decided to buy five more copies, one for each of my "Tribe," my closest girlfriends, for Christmas. It reminded me so much of us."

Women United Rock "I love this novel about mid-life women connecting and re-connecting no matter how many years they are apart. Any women could find bits of themselves in each of these characters. So many women go thru early life pitting themselves against one another. This story speaks of women who build and maintain relationships and there are so many of us who live this story. Great read."

Couldn't Put it Down "Couldn't put this book down. I didn't want it to end. The characters and plot were well developed, and I felt like I knew them at the end. I hope there is a sequel so I can see what happens next."

ACKNOWLEDGMENTS

Thank you to my advance readers Terry Gold, Sandy Foulkes, Rob Robbins, Robbie Bos, and Tami Walker. To my critique group, Rommy Nelson, and Lori Carson … I appreciate your invaluable suggestions and support.

Thank you to Dr. David Horner, MD, for your medical insights into Lizzy's condition.

A shout-out to the folks at Big City Jiu-Jitsu for teaching me the techniques that I referred to in the book.

A special thank you to my cover models Lisa Patterson and Rae Skyler Walker.

And finally, thank you to Karene Horst of Flying Trees Publishing for her final edits and support.

"The dog was the first animal domesticated by Homo Sapiens. Dogs were used for hunting and fighting and as an alarm system against wild beasts and human intruders. With the passing of the generations, the two species co-evolved to communicate well with each other. Dogs that were most attentive to the needs and feelings of their human companions got extra care and food and were more likely to survive. Simultaneously, dogs learned to manipulate people for their own needs. A 15,000-year-old bond has yielded a much deeper understanding and affection between humans and dogs than between humans and any other animal."

Sapiens, a brief history of humankind, by Yuval Noah Harari

"I had a wonderful teacher about animal behavior—my dog Rusty. He taught me that animals have personalities, minds, and feelings."

Jane Goodall

Chapter One

Stomp Clap – No

Aren't we a pair? My dog Rae has but one functioning ear, while I can only speak in a barely audible whisper. Together we live in a world of hand signals and murmurs, barks and whines.

Woof.

A sigh escapes my lips as I type, "Hold on," then hit send. Walking through the kitchen to the back door, I pull my oversized sweater/coat tighter in preparation for the blast of frigid air. With my cell phone on the table, speaker on, my mother's voice follows me into the kitchen.

"That dog wants in again? What is that? The tenth time?"

The sixth, but who's counting.

"You should put in one of those doggie doors. They aren't that …"

Doggie doors in the mountains are an open invitation to raccoons, skunks, and squirrels looking for a free meal. I've told her this before, but she doesn't remember.

When I open the back door, my energetic ball of black and white fur rushes inside along with a gust of air filled with face-stinging icy crystals. The first day of March is living up to the adage, "in like a lion." I shut the door quickly, giving my full attention to the shag carpet on four legs shaking like the butt-giggling twerkers on YouTube. Whether I've been gone for hours or minutes, her welcome is always the same. It fills me with joy.

Bending over, I give my little Rae of sunshine a vigorous two-handed bottom scratch before slapping my thigh three times, the signal for "follow me," which she does. As we return to the dining table that is currently my office, Rae's tail is still wagging. Now, it's more like a metronome than a helicopter, the straight white hair at the tip of her tail waving like a surrendering flag.

Half poodle (the smart part) and half Bernese Mountain Dog (the cuddly part), Rae is a mid-size model Doodle with long wavy black hair that tends to morph into dreadlocks if I don't brush her often. She has four white knee socks, a white chest and muzzle. Her caramel brown eyes peek out from under a curtain of black that I trim often so she can see.

Mom hasn't stopped talking—something about a new guy … her latest flavor of the month.

"I'm back," I text before sitting. The table is covered with seed catalogs and a half dozen yellow legal pads, each one holding important ideas for different areas of my life … the community garden, the newsletters I'm writing, trips I want to take, and my favorite, random thoughts. Writing on notepads is so baby boomer. My peers have their notes on their phones or computers. Ever since I was robbed of my voice, I've been forced to text or write to communicate. Reverting to the pre-computer practice of putting pen to paper has become a pleasant break from my sad reality.

Mom hasn't acknowledged that I was gone and continues her story while Rae moves under the table to lie on my feet. I love that she wants to be close, and it has the added bonus of keeping my feet warm. I wonder what's in it for her?

I love lying on her feet. On any part of her. No matter where she is, I like touching her. Sometimes I sit and lean against her leg. When she is lying down, I curl up next to her … my favorite. I can feel her breathing. I can tell a lot about how she is feeling. By the rhythm of her breath. The beat of her heart. She is soft. I like the way she smells.

While mom continues her soliloquy, I check email (mostly spam). Check the weather (two inches of snow expected). Scroll through my favorite news apps (surprise … the world is going to shit).

Her question, "Lizzy. Are you still there?" breaks through my thoughts.

I text, "Yes."

"Okay good. I thought I'd lost you like before. Pine City needs to invest in more cell towers. You should write a letter to the

City Council or the local newspaper ..."

And she's off. A letter to the editor. Right. For the entire community to read. And people off-mountain, too, since this is a tourist town. While I'm at it, I could take out an ad, "Lizzy has moved to Pine City." Sometimes I think Mom has forgotten why I moved up here in the first place.

Rae jerks to attention.

What's that? Chattering. Squirrel. That squirrel is bad. I must warn her. Woof, woof, woof. I'm not sure where he is. Is he in the house? I turn my head this way. I turn my head that way. The chattering is strong in one ear, but not in the other. I need to turn my head until the sound is strong in my good ear.

Scrambling to move out from under the table and through the chair legs, Rae races around the living room, to the front door, then the back door, barking as she runs. She hears a squirrel but because she's deaf in one ear, she is not sure where the little tormentor is hiding. And while Rae can hear the smallest sounds like the ping of my phone or the psst sound I use to draw her attention, she needs two functioning ears to triangulate where the sound is coming from.

Rae continues barking at the chattering creature. I would like to yell, "No!" But I can't. Instead, I stomp my foot and clap my hands. She looks at me and barks again. I stomp and clap.

I do not like the stomp clap. It means she wants me to stop what I'm doing. Doesn't she know that there is a squirrel somewhere? My job is to let her know. My job is to keep her safe.

Stomp and clap. Rae drops her head and flops down on the floor in defeat with an audible disgruntled sigh.

Woof.

She always gets the last word.

"What is all that commotion? Is that dog barking again? I don't know how you stand it. It's one of the things I hated about the commune ... all those dogs. They didn't belong to anyone but sort of belonged to everyone. They just wandered around unsupervised."

Sort of like us children. "It's a squirrel that's making her bark," I text.

"A squirrel. Don't they carry rabies?"

Wow. She's actually reading my text. "No. Not squirrels."

When I first moved to the mountains, I read an article about raccoons and skunks carrying rabies. Another reason not to have a doggie door.

"Some people think squirrels are cute, but I don't like them. They are furry rats. They found their way into everything at The Farm ..."

The Farm. That wasn't the official name for the commune near Eureka where I lived the first fourteen years of my life, but that's what Mom and I call it. How did my mother survive living with all the animals and kids running free? Or maybe that's *why* she doesn't like animals. Twenty-four years later, looking back through the eyes of an adult, I'm guessing it was all the free love.

The alarm goes off on my phone. Oh good. A reason to escape.

"Mom. I've gotta run. I'm meeting someone for tea." Hitting send, I wait for her reply. Nothing. Slipping the phone into my back pocket, Mom continues talking, her voice now muffled. Although she drives me crazy with her never-ending monologues, hanging up on her feels mean.

I change into boots, wrap a white scarf around my neck and pull on a white wool hat before wrestling into my long, black puffy jacket. The moment Rae's leash comes off the hook, she starts spinning in circles, toenails clicking on the hardwood floor creating the music for her happy dance. Snapping my fingers, she sits and waits—a quivering, barely-contained ball of energy. As soon as I finish hooking the leash to her collar, she lunges for the door. Grabbing my daypack, I brace for the cold.

Going for a walk. I love walks. No. Not a walk. A ride. I love rides. My girl opens the door to the car. I leap onto the seat. I go everywhere with my girl. Sometimes I stay in here alone, but never for very long. She always comes back. I look out through the clear wall. White fluffy flakes are moving everywhere. Those trees. The ones that smell like something I can eat. Those trees are shaking. White flakes move through the air. They hit the clear wall. The black blades swish back and forth. The white flakes are being pushed away. I stand up. My eyes follow the blades. Ruff. My girl twitters. I wait for the blade to come back. Ruff. My girl makes the shhhh sound with a finger to her lips. The blade comes back. Ruff.

One more shhhh. I curl up on the seat with my head on her leg. I am rewarded with a scratch behind my ears.

Silly dog, barking at the windshield wipers. I back out of the driveway in my nondescript white Honda and head to Keri's Place, a log cabin converted into a tea and coffee joint. Because it's tucked away in a residential neighborhood, the place doesn't attract tourist hordes or many strangers. Something I appreciate. Normally I would have walked, since it's only a half-mile from my house, but not in this weather. Rae would have loved it, though. With her thick fur coat, she can stay outside in the snow for hours.

My only close friend in Pine City is meeting me at Keri's after she drops her kids off at softball and baseball practice. Abby will have two hours before she needs to pick them up. I've met her kids a few times. While being around babies has me reaching for a tissue and hiding in the closest bathroom to cry, older children don't have the same effect on me.

Abby's children are always more excited to see Rae than me, which is understandable. Rae is the fun one while I'm the quiet one.
The girl, Samantha, calls Rae, "The Muppet." The boy, Dylan, calls her "Rags." Both names are appropriate for a shaggy dog. Nobody knows the real name of my dog. If I can't shout her name when I want her to come, then I don't want other people to be able to call her either.

Abby's white Subaru, the unofficial car of the mountains, isn't parked out front as I pull up to Keri's Place. Rae pops up. I don't know how, but she knows where we are.

Treats. This place has treats. Sometimes crunchy. Sometimes chewy. When the door opens, I leap out. I pull my girl up the cold path ignoring the interesting smells in the grass on either side. I ignore the cold white flakes in the air. People come out the door. A man who smells like smoke holds the door open for my girl. I pull her through and up to the tall counter where the treats await. I sit without the snap and lift my nose into the air. There are three kinds of treats here. My favorite treat has meat, carrots, and potatoes. I look for the girl who smells like another dog. She is my favorite. She is the one who greets me with happy sounds. She always has a treat ready for me. The boy who smells like a cat is okay. I make the low rrrrrrrr sound in my throat. I want a treat. Rrrrrrrr.

Sometimes I regret teaching my dog to talk. That is what she is doing, or thinks she is doing. When she makes the soft *rrrrrrrr* sound it means she wants her breakfast, her lunch, her dinner, or a treat. Some people mistake the sound for a growl. It's not. Her mouth is closed. Her eyes are bright. Her ears are perky. It's not a growl. I make the *rrrrrrrr* sound too, although not as well. I bring the sound up at the end to indicate a question such as, "Do you want breakfast?" She answers with a more enthusiastic rrrrrrrr, head tilted back, throat stretched tautly. It's almost a howl.

Most of the people at Keri's understand what she is saying. Keri, the owner, and a dog person, usually comes out from behind the counter, which was built three feet in front of the kitchen door in this house conversion. She makes Rae sit, shake, then lie down before giving her a treat. Once the treat is gone, she gives Rae a good bottom scratch. Carl, the cat owner, always hands me the treat over the top of the counter.

Carl, the barely-out-of-high-school-isn't-going-to-college guy is working today. He doesn't see or hear Rae, or maybe he takes pleasure in ignoring her. I must point down at the dog, then to the treat jar. Rae tries to help by making the *rrrrrrrr* again. You'd think he'd know by now that my dog is always with me, and she always wants a treat. He also doesn't remember my order, even though I have the same thing every time. Chai tea latte, with low-fat milk and cinnamon. I haven't decided if he's stupid or just doesn't care that much. Probably a little of both.

My girl points to the treat jar. The lid makes a "tink" sound when the boy opens it. Before I see the treat, I know which one it is. I sit without the snap. My girl gives me the treat. I wag my tail.

Pulling my phone out of my back pocket, I type my order and show it to Carl. He looks at me oddly. Guess he doesn't remember that I don't speak.

Moments later, with my hot drink in one hand, and Rae's leash in the other, I walk through the dining room area, which is a quiet zone for people working on laptops. Rae pulls me along to the large living room. The room oozes comfort with its cozy chairs, mismatched couches, and a river rock floor-to-ceiling fireplace that currently has a roaring fire throwing off warm,

17

delicious, heat. The couch and overstuffed chairs closest to the fireplace have all been taken so I find an empty loveseat and coffee table in the far corner with a view of the front door. On the rare occasion that I'm in a public place, I always sit with a clear view of the door. Coat, hat, and scarf draped on a chair, I pull out my tablet and wait. Abby is usually late. Rae reluctantly lies at my feet with an audible sigh, which I recognize as her discontented harrumph sigh, not her contented ahhh sigh.

I want to jump up and lie down next to my girl. Put my head on her leg. Then she will rub my ears. But this couch is a clap stomp thing. We have a couch at our house. At our house, she pats the soft cushions. I jump up. She is happy when I put my head on her leg. I cannot do that here. Here I must stay on the ground. I don't understand. When I sit and lean into her leg, she rubs my ears. I push my head into her hand. This is good but not as good as being on the couch next to her. I moan, letting her know she is doing a good job. She should keep rubbing.

Ten minutes later, Abby comes through the door, a dusting of snowflakes clinging to her curly brown hair. Abby does a quick scan of the living room, her gaze going right over me without a hint of recognition. Several men stop mid-conversation, at the sight of Abby's ample curves. Watching their reaction makes me appreciate being short and flat-chested, which helps me go unnoticed … essential when you're hiding out.

Abby turns and heads to the kitchen. Moments later, she is standing at the entrance to the living room again, hot coffee in hand, looking for me. I wave. She does a literal double-take. Surprisingly, she doesn't give herself whiplash or spill her coffee.

She rushes over. "Oh my god, Lizzy. I didn't recognize you."
Setting her coffee on the small wooden table stained with coffee rings, she gives Rae a quick pet before sitting next to me, her eyes never leaving my face.

"Your hair! It's so different. The color. The cut. Wow! When did you do this?"

My tablet is ready. I type, "Six weeks ago. You like it?"

Abby's smile and small excited hand claps say everything. "I love, love, love it."

Abby looks at Rae for the first time and then back at me. "All you need is a streak of white added to your jet-black hair and you two could be twins."

That's funny. I hadn't thought about that. I type. "Not my intention, but I see what you mean."

Abby drinks her coffee as she reads. "What do you call the cut?" she asks.

"An A-Bob. It's shorter in the back," I type, then turn my head showing off the hairstyle.

"Very classy. What prompted the change?"

Now it's my turn to do the excited hand claps, which Rae mistakes as her signal to come, which it is, but that wasn't my intention. She springs onto the couch and sits between Abby and me, her eyes bright, tail thumping. I clap and stomp, pointing to the floor. Rae's head drops as she reluctantly climbs back down, first one foot, then the other, all at a fraction of the speed it took her to climb up here. She lies down, curls up on my feet, and lets out a loud harrumph-like sigh. I lean over and give her a good rub to let her know I still love her before typing my answer for Abby.

"Look at this," I type before pulling my driver's license out of my wallet.

My picture shows a woman with short, raven-black hair, a pale complexion, and heavy, dark eyeshadow. I'm wearing a shiny black leather jacket. I look very Goth. The most important thing … I look nothing like my former self.

"Wow."

Then I point to the name.

"Lizzy Mueller? You changed your name, too?"

I nod, feeling very proud and clever. When I filed for divorce from Charlie, I filled out the forms to change my name at the same time. Instead of going back to my maiden name, which would be easy to trace, I took my father's last name. The father that was supposedly dead and Charlie didn't know existed.

"You decided to take Frank's name?"

I nod.

"Does Frank know?

Shaking my head I type, "I'm going to surprise him. Do you think he'll like that we now share the same name?"

"You mean the father who buried a dead body to keep his daughter out of jail? That father? Of course, he'll be thrilled."

Once the "crime" at the community garden had been solved and the story broke in the local paper, everyone, at least everyone at the garden, knew Frank was my father. Considering I had just found out myself made things weird. Thinking about how Berta, the community garden know-it-all died, makes me feel nervous all over again. Her death was a tragedy, turned mystery, and a huge story in our tiny mountain community. Did the local story make it into one of the larger papers off the hill? Will Charlie be able to use the information to track me down?

Something is wrong. Lizzy is shaking. I can feel it in her feet. I sit up and put a paw on her leg. She doesn't respond. I make the high-pitched whine that means I'm scared, or nervous because I am scared, scared for my girl. She puts her warm drink on the table and takes my head in her hands and scratches behind my ears. She is still shaking. I want to jump on her lap and lick her face. I want to make her better. She slaps the cushion and I'm up in an instant. She pulls me onto her lap and puts her arms around me. I lick her hand until she stops trembling.

"No dogs on the furniture," Carl tosses out the comment as he walks around the living room collecting empty cups and wadded-up napkins.

Apparently, he cares more about the couch than remembering what customers order.

Abby looks up. "The dog is on her lap, technically not on the couch," she says, shooing him away with her hand as if he were an annoying mosquito before returning her attention to the tablet.

"I still find it unbelievable that Frank is your dad. I knew there was something strange about the way he treated you. I thought—" Abby says with a tilt of her head and a wicked twinkle in her eye, "—that he had a crush on you."

Me, too, I mouth.

"He was always finding excuses to talk to you. But your father? Didn't see that coming. And you didn't either? What are the odds? You move to Pine City and join the exact community garden where your father, a father you didn't even know you had, is the garden steward? It's like a movie or magic or something."

Throwing my hands in the air, I lift my shoulders as if to say, right? But it wasn't a coincidence or magic. It was a carefully orchestrated plan by my sneaky mother who, to give her credit, was trying her best to protect me from my crazy husband.

"It's all so unbelievable. Did I say unbelievable before?"

I smile and nod.

"Right, but it's just so…"

Unbelievable, I mouth, and we both burst into laughter.

Abby's laugh is a loud bray like a horse neighing. My laugh is more of a disquieting cackle like the sound of hens laying their eggs if … the hens were being strangled. Rae freaks and leaps off my lap as we draw stares from other people in the room. Not good. The first rule of hiding out is, "Do not draw attention to yourself."

I put my hand over my mouth to stop the disturbing sounds.

Typing … "But seriously, I'm trying to downplay the fact that Frank is my father, especially at the garden or anywhere in public, for that matter. Once people knew that Berta wasn't actually murdered, they lost interest in the story. I'm grateful that they kept my photo out of the newspaper. That could have been a disaster."

Abby looks at what I've written and nods, the giggles squashed. "Is that why you changed your looks?"

I nod.

"Regardless of the reason, you look amazing."

That makes me smile and I sign, "Thanks."

For the next hour, Abby catches me up on what's happening with her, as the snow keeps falling quietly outside. I love hearing about her ordinary life. Yeah, she's divorced and has to deal with her jerk-of-an-ex-husband, but for the most part, her life is about normal stuff. Stuff that I thought I'd be doing by now like taking care of children, cooking meals for my family, putting together photo albums and baby books of every significant moment in my children's lives.

I'd always yearned for a traditional family as opposed to how I was raised—with multiple father figures, and dozens of siblings and dogs. I pictured a family with one mom, one dad, two or three children, and definitely a dog or two. We'd all live in a regular house and the kids would go to a regular school and we'd all have nice boring lives. A boring life … sounds perfect. At thirty-eight, I feel I'm running out of time to make that dream come true. At least I have my dog.

"Hey, we should get going. It's getting pretty thick out there," Abby says as she stands.

She's right. In the last hour, a solid two inches of snow has collected against the windows. Rae pops up, tail wagging, apparently ready to go as well. I bundle up again before heading to the door. Abby and I say our goodbyes inside before we open the door to a blast of cold air filled with soft white flakes.

Four hours later, dinner and dishes done, I'm sitting on the couch reading a mystery with Rae beside me, her head on my lap, as the storm intensifies outside. I have a fire going, but it's having trouble keeping up with the steady drop in temperature. Rae doesn't know how to tell time, but every night, a couple of hours after the sun goes down, she stands and trots to my bedroom door, pauses, looking back at me as if to say, "Come on. It's bedtime."

Tonight, she heads to the bedroom at eight-fifty. Some nights I stay up longer and read, but on nights like tonight, I think she might have a point. I leave my book on the coffee table, check the locks on the doors then turn off the lights. The glow of the porch light coming through the front window is enough to help me navigate safely to the bedroom. Rae is already curled up in a ball positioned in the center of the bed.

It takes five minutes to change into flannel PJs, brush my teeth and hair, and use the toilet. When I pull back the covers, that's Rae's signal. She waits for me to crawl into bed then repositions herself, so she is sleeping in the curve of my belly.

Before switching off the lamp next to my bed, I stare at the two framed bird paintings hanging on the wall at the foot of the bed. The larger painting is of a bird with purple plumage caught in mid-flight. The smaller painting features a sparkling blue hummingbird perched on a branch. The birds glow and shimmer in the warm incandescent light making them come alive. Looking at the paintings, a sad longing makes my chest ache. The paintings are there so I'll never forget. Taking a deep breath, I turn off the lamp. Rae makes a huffing sound because I have disturbed her. With my arm draped over my dog, I relax, letting the rise and fall of her chest lure me to sleep. Rae will stay with me for a while before jumping off the bed to do whatever it is she does while I sleep.

My girl is breathing deeply, a faint whistle comes from her mouth. I jump off the bed and walk through the house, my toenails clicking on the wooden floor. Jumping on the couch, I stand with my front feet on the back of the couch. Now I can look through the clear wall. The white flakes are bigger now. They glow in the light coming from the tall light pole where all the dogs in the neighborhood mark their place. I watch but nothing else is moving. No people are walking with my four-legged friends. No cars are moving. It is so quiet, just like my girl, my quiet girl. Satisfied that all is right, I circle around and around and around until I'm a tight little ball, my tail tucked in just right, my nose under my paw.

The dream jolts me awake, a ragged cry escaping my lips. My cry sounds like the growl of a troll under a bridge warning people away. If anyone were to hear me scream, they would not come running to save this damsel in distress but turn and run. But Rae has come. Rae is here. She bounds onto the bed and curls against my belly, tilting her head back so she can lick my throat as if she knows this is where the trauma took place. Three years ago, my husband wrapped his hands around my throat and strangled me until my vision went black and the high-pitched buzzing in my head went silent along with my voice.

Chapter Two

Six Years Ago – June

It was unseasonably warm for June, and of course, that's when the air conditioner in the kitchen at Saint Bridget's Hospital decided to take the day off. While the maintenance guys tried to fix the problem, I had a couple of floor fans brought in to move the torrid air around. The kitchen staff was as grumpy and uncomfortable as Satan's house cat.

It was right after the final lunches had been delivered that Nurse Cooper stuck her head in the kitchen door.

"Is Lizzy in here?" I heard her call.

Gary, the head chef, pointed in my direction where I sat at my desk reviewing the meal plans for the coming week.

"The patient in room 112 wants to give his compliments to the chef," Nurse Cooper said.

"Gary's the chef," I responded before returning to the task at hand.

"He specifically said, he wants to meet the person, who created, and I quote, 'these restaurant-quality meals.'"

"Well, there he is," I said, pointing back at Gary.

Gary shook his head. "I just follow your recipes and meal plans. Any idiot could do that. You should go. Besides, I need to start prepping for dinner."

I gave Nurse Cooper a grimace as I stood.

"Hey, I'm just the messenger," she shrugged before adding, "Room 112. And if it helps, he's cute."

It didn't help at all. I hadn't had a boyfriend in years and wasn't actively looking, but a patient was a customer, so I reluctantly stood up.

"Fine."

Minutes later, I stood at the open door of room 112. The patient was staring out the window of his private room and hadn't noticed me. This guy must have been in one hell of an accident. The cast on his left leg covered his foot to above his knee, all of which was being suspended two feet in the air by the pulley system over his bed. His right arm also in a cast, was plastered into place in the form of someone holding up a stop sign. That had to be uncomfortable. The bandage that wound around his forehead made the bleached-blonde hair sticking out below the bandage look like a ballerina's tutu.

Cute? How could you tell? I thought, as I knocked lightly

on the door, then waited.

When he turned toward me, I had my answer. Crystal blue eyes, a bronze tan, and a smile that slid up to the corner of his eyes making you feel like you were the center of his world.

"Hi," he said with an enthusiasm that belied his current condition.

"Hi." I took a step into the room. "What happened to you?"

He shrugged, which must have hurt because he winced, before saying, "Car versus skateboard."

"Wow. If you're this banged up, what happened to the skateboarder?"

With his good arm, he made a grand gesture. "You're looking at him."

"You're the skateboarder?"

"Yep," he nodded.

"Aren't you a bit old to be riding a skateboard?" I guessed his age to be in his mid-thirties.

"My parents certainly think so, but don't tell that to the Birdman," he said with that killer smile aimed directly at me like a heat-seeking missile.

"Who?"

"Thirty-eight-year-old Tony Hawk, the richest professional skater in the world. He's made millions. While I don't have professional aspirations … I'm more into surfing … I do enjoy a good ride."

How did I get sucked into a conversation about

skateboarding? Let's find out what he wanted to say about the food so I can return to work.

"I'm Lizzy, by the way, the hospital's nutritionist. I plan all the meals and create the recipes. Nurse Cooper said you wanted to see me."

"Oh my god, yes. Come in. Come in."

I took a few more steps into the room until I was about three feet from his bed.

"Closer. I don't bite," he said playfully.

Closing the distance, I was now standing close enough to notice the abrasions on his uninjured arm.

"I had to tell you in person. The food here is amazing ... five stars. The best, and not just for a hospital, but better than some restaurants. And I've been to a lot of restaurants. So, you're the one responsible for these awesome meals?"

I nodded. In the last four years, I'd never had a patient request to see me, let alone call my meals "awesome." I was at a loss for words, but this guy wasn't.

"The beef stroganoff was rich with flavor, and the mushrooms weren't overcooked and limp. Definitely fresh. Not from a can. I could taste the wine in the sauce, something I was surprised to find in a hospital meal. Most hospitals will say beef stroganoff on the menu but what it turns out to be is overcooked noodles, hamburger, mixed with mushroom soup." He made a gagging sound for emphasis. "Your stroganoff is the real deal."

"I picked the pot roast for dinner tonight with broccoli and potatoes, and the cheesecake for dessert. I bet the broccoli will be steamed to perfection, not boiled."

I nodded. Who was this guy? A food critic?

"What's for dinner tomorrow?" he wanted to know.

"Tomorrow is Taco Tuesday. Veggie tacos with fresh guacamole and chips."

"Dang. They said they're releasing me tomorrow morning. Maybe I can stay long enough for lunch. What's for lunch?"

"Don't you want to leave here as quickly as possible?" Most people do, I thought.

"Well, sure. But I'd hate to miss one of your meals. They are delightful."

Who says, "delightful," I thought before answering. "If I remember right, lunch is Italian meatball sandwiches with fresh coleslaw, although the meatballs are plant-based. Tasty but healthy, that's my goal."

"I'm staying for sure," he said with a laugh. "Meatball sandwiches are my favorite."

"That's great," I said before sneaking a glance at the clock on the wall. "Well, it was nice meeting you. I need to get back to work."

"Oh, I forgot. What's for breakfast? Today I had French Toast, and it was amazing. Real maple syrup, too, right?"

I nodded.

"I knew it."

I took a step back, trying to ease my way out of the room

and the conversation. "If I remember right, tomorrow's breakfast is banana pancakes with fruit."

"Yum." He paused then asked, "Will I see you again before I'm discharged tomorrow?"

"Probably not. My job doesn't have much interaction with the patients."

His smile faded. "That's too bad. I'd like to get to know more about the person who can turn hospital food into a gourmet experience."

"Maybe you'll have another accident and end up back here," I said jokingly, taking another step closer to the door.

"I can only hope," he said and blew me a kiss.

I laughed before turning and leaving the room. Nurse Cooper was right. He was kind of cute after all.

Two weeks later, a bouquet of white roses showed up in the hospital kitchen, an apparent first, based on the buzz it caused among the staff. The accompanying note said, "I do want to get to know you better, but I'm not willing to crash and burn again to do it. If you'd like to meet for coffee or drinks, here's my number. Charlie."

Funny, until the flowers came, I didn't even know his name.

After a dozen dates, Charlie wanted me to meet his parents. To be more accurate, his parents had insisted on meeting me. I knew his family was rich (I'd Googled them) but when we pulled up to their estate in south Orange County, I let my shock escape by blurting out, "Holy shit." I had no idea that castles existed outside of Europe.

"I know, right? It's a bit much. But you ain't seen nothing yet. I hope you don't hold my mother's extravagances against me," Charlie said, reaching over and squeezing my hand before driving up the cobblestone horseshoe driveway that must have been a half-mile long if it were a yard. The center of the horseshoe was filled with two-foot-high sculptured hedges that made an intricate pattern leading up to, then encircling, a stone fountain.

Charlie looked where I was staring. "Isn't it cool? It's a maze. You enter at the end of the driveway, and if you choose correctly, you'll wind up at the fountain. My brother Phillip and I used the maze to play war games, much to our mother's disapproval."

"Sounds like fun," I said, still working on keeping my mouth from hanging open in awe.

As we approached the front entrance, I had to crane my neck backward to take in the entire house.

"I'm supposed to park around the corner at the seven-bay car stable," Charlie said in a conspiratorial whisper.

Then mimicking a stern, imperial voice he continued, "Cars littering the driveway …"
then in a whisper, "especially my car … spoils the first impression of those arriving at the estate."

We pulled up slightly past the front door and Charlie put

his lovingly restored 1950 Ford Woody—the history of which I'd heard about on our last date—into park and asked me to wait. He jumped out and ran around to open the door for me, holding out his hand to assist my exit.

"Babe, wait 'til we go inside … as a kid, I thought it was pretty cool. It wasn't all warm and cozy, but we made do. The marble floors were cold but made for a smooth racing surface for our Hot Wheels, and the high vaulted ceilings gave Phillip and me all the room we needed to fly paper airplanes, although when they got tangled in the chandelier we'd run like hell. Our favorite thing to do was to slide down the banisters of the twin staircase. Phillip would climb on one, I on the other, and we'd race to the bottom. The two staircases curved into each other, so sometimes we'd pop off the railing and slam into each other. It was all good fun unless mother caught us. Then we'd run like hell out the front door and hide in the maze."

I couldn't help thinking of my childhood. Dirt instead of marble floors, open skies instead of a vaulted ceiling, and a couple of tarps and a hose for sliding down a hill.

Charlie didn't open the door but pressed a discreet button that was hidden in the wrought iron embellishments that matched the front doors.

"You can't just walk in? This *is* your house, right?"

Charlie shook his head. "This is my mother's house, and we must be announced."

He gave my hand a reassuring squeeze before continuing.

"Look. My mother is a bit pretentious … very pretentious when you first meet her. My dad is more of a regular Joe. He'll love you. But it's my mother who is *lord* of this castle. I want her to like you so here are a few tips. Ignore all of this," he said, waving his free hand to encompass the front entrance.

"Don't compliment her looks, the food, the tea, the décor. Don't look around in awe as if you've never seen such splendor. All your compliments will be lumped into one category … sucking up. She despises people who try to ingratiate themselves. Just imagine that we are having a chai tea latte at Jack's Coffee Shack, the ocean waves gently rolling up onto the sand."

Before we arrived, my stomach was already doing somersaults and tumbles at the prospect of meeting Charlie's famous parents. After all, they were the wealthiest individual property owners in California with an estimated net worth of 9.5 BILLION dollars! But now, listening to Charlie's instructions for meeting his mother, I was ready to hightail it out of there. I turned away from the door pulling Charlie's hand as I took my first step.

"Let's go. We can meet your family another day."

Charlie pulled me back. "Babe, it'll be fine. Just be yourself. I love you," he said, pulling me in closer, then planting a warm kiss on my lips.

Suddenly everything stopped. The grandeur of the house and the terror of the moment took a back seat to those three little words … I love you. He'd never said them before. As my mouth pulled away from his, I was able to whisper, "I love you, too," before the front door swung open.

"Master Bouchard," a warm, cultured voice greeted us.

Now in addition to being a nervous wreck, I flushed red with embarrassment at being caught in an intimate embrace.

"Hey Mac," Charlie said with the same casual air he used to greet his surfer buddies. "This is Lizzy."

"Charmed," Mac said with a slight bow, his black and white butler's uniform barely letting him bow at all. "Your mother is waiting in the garden room."

As we walked under the giant crystal chandelier hanging over the center of the foyer, I made sure I didn't look up. Continuing down a hallway that was as wide as my mother's living room, my eyes moved from left to right like a retro black and white cat clock, taking in all the portraits that lined the antique white stone walls. We walked past several ornate doors, all closed to hide their secrets, on our journey to the garden room. Although the floor was marble, our approach was silent due to a long-patterned rug that ran down the middle of the hall, probably Persian.

Finally, we arrived. I quashed a tremendous urge to check my step count on my phone's health app. The journey from the front door to this room alone must have moved me toward my 8,000 daily step goal. I squeezed Charlie's hand instead.

Charlie bent his head close to mine, and whispered in my ear, "I forgot to tell you about the tea. Only take one cube of sugar and no cream. Mother disapproves of people who add unnecessary additions to her expensive imported brews."

Charlie gave my hand another squeeze before pulling free of my death grip. Suddenly, I didn't know what to do with my arms.

"Master Bouchard and Miss Lizzy," Mac announced.

Sitting on the front edge of a brocade high-backed chair, back ramrod straight, head held high, a magazine resting on her lap, was the impeccably dressed Mrs. Catherine Elenore McKinzie Bouchard, wife of Robert Michael Bouchard, mother of the late Phillip Michael Bouchard, and my boyfriend, Charles Michael Bouchard.

What have I gotten myself into? I thought, resisting the urge to curtsy.

Mrs. Bouchard rose without effort to greet us. Tall, thin, and regal, were my first impressions. Her long thin fingers were lightly clasped in front of her as we walked into the brightly lit room that I dared not look at in awe. Charlie's mother's blonde-as-vanilla-ice-cream hair was pulled into a bun at the back of her long neck, with purposeful loose tendrils framing her face, a face that serenely watched my every move like a cat watches a bird.

Giving Charlie's mom my most winning smile, I followed Charlie into the room. My smile was not returned but I refused to look away. If she was going to study me like I was something she was about to eat, then I was going to study her right back.

Her blue eyes had none of the merriment like Charlie's. They were the color of an approaching storm, hiding bolts of lightning and claps of thunder. Those stormy eyes looked me up and down over a long thin nose. When I didn't turn away from her penetrating assessment, the slightest of smiles curled up the corners of her thin mouth. Her golden tan was so smooth and perfect that I suspected it had been sprayed on.

An eggshell white, one-piece, long-sleeved pantsuit, flowed over her long legs, falling to the floor like a skirt. Her perfectly manicured toes sticking out from under the waves of soft fabric surprised me.

No shoes. Interesting. Either she wasn't as uptight as she seemed, or she didn't want to dirty the rectangle of white shaggy carpet that covered the floor in front of her chair and the couch. Probably the latter.

A thin gold belt accentuated her tiny waist and matched the gold necklace around her throat. This casual outfit must have cost thousands, which made me feel self-conscious in my Nordstrom Rack wrap dress and strappy low heels.

"Charles. Miss Lizzy. Please come in and have a seat." She gestured to the matching brocade settee that faced the French doors offering the best view of the garden.

Then she turned to Mac. "You can bring in the tea, now."

Twenty minutes later, I was choking down my second cup of barely sweetened tea. The bitter tea tasted like leaves … not a good type of tea leaves, but like leaves raked in the fall and stuffed in giant plastic bags. The conversation so far had been fairly *droll,* with Mrs. Bouchard asking me the usual polite questions…where I'd gone to school, where I worked. The majority of questions were aimed at Charlie. It was all very polite and proper, so I was unprepared for the question that came next.

"Miss Stewart. What do you think of people who have an obscene amount of money?"

Whoa. I paused. Tell the truth or give a socially acceptable answer? To hell with it. I was tired of sitting up straight and sipping her expensive weird-tasting tea.

"You have to understand, I grew up in a commune. A dozen fathers, a dozen mothers, and a pack of wild children. This …" I said gesturing to the sitting room that was larger than my mother's entire house, "is as foreign to me as walking on the moon. Frankly, I don't know what to think about any of it." With that, I scooted closer to Charlie until our thighs were touching. I tucked my arm under his, and took his hand in mine, before smiling sweetly at Charlie's mother.

There was a deadly silence for five beats of my heart. Charlie had stopped breathing and gone stiff as a cardboard cutout until Catherine burst into laughter. I looked at Charlie and he finally took a deep breath before we looked back at his mother. When her laughter sputtered to a halt, she used a cloth handkerchief to daintily wipe the corners of her eyes.

"Finally," she said to Charlie. "You brought home a woman with an honest streak. Good for you, Charlie." And then to me. "I like you, Miss Stewart—"

"Lizzy. Please call me Lizzy," I interrupted.

"Okay, Lizzy," she said with a sigh before rearranging

herself in her chair, tucking her bare feet under her.

I squeezed Charlie's hand before standing up. "Bathroom? I hear you have a dozen of them."

Catherine laughed lightly pointing toward the door. "Turn left. Third door on your right."

The bathroom, a tomb of dark wood and gilded frames of pastoral scenes, made me feel claustrophobic. At least the toilet wasn't gold. Walking back, I took my time, looking at the framed paintings that lined the hallway. I stopped in front of a family portrait that was probably seven feet tall. Catherine looked eerily the same … tall, regal, hair the same color and style. Her husband stood next to her. He had a kind, soft face, with Charlie's pale blue eyes and a friendly dimple. He stood slightly taller than Catherine, his dark brown hair slicked back. He wore a pleasant smile and a pale gray suit, a white shirt, with a red cravat.

Two small boys stood in front of their parents also in miniature suits, a darker shade of gray than their father's. The taller of the two, I assumed, was Phillip. He had his father's dark hair and his mother's dark eyes, a very serious expression on his cupid face as he held his little brother's hand.

Charlie looked to be about two. The artist had captured the sparkle in his eyes, the barely contained mischief that lurked beneath his childish grin, and a head of blonde curls that made him look like an angel. Each parent had a hand resting on Phillip's shoulder, while Charlie was only attached to Phillip and a cat that was leaning against his leg.

NO WORDS BETWEEN US

Based on what Charlie had told me about his place in the family, it was easy to see that Phillip was the heir apparent. Charlie had regaled me with tales of his childhood, often relating the escapades of Phillip and Charlie and the mischief they created. Whenever they got caught, Catherine always assumed that Charlie was the instigator even though he was the younger brother. Phillip never said anything to make her believe otherwise.

When Phillip was twenty-one, he died in a car crash. He was reportedly going 120 miles per hour driving home from Las Vegas. Charlie was away at college. For once, Catherine couldn't blame Charlie.

Continuing down the hall looking at other paintings, I heard Catherine raise her voice. Stopping short of the sitting room door, I held my breath as I listened.

"Have you asked her about children?"

"Jesus Christ, Mother. That's totally uncool."

"Please talk like an adult. Listen. You seem to like this one but why waste your time with someone who doesn't want children? How old is she, anyway? Thirty-eight?"

Thirty-eight? I turned and looked into one of the many gilded mirrors in the hallway. Do I look that old?

"She's thirty-two." Charlie sounded as offended as I felt.

"That's good. She has about six good child-bearing years left. Plenty of time to have at least three kids."

Seriously, lady. Three kids? Anything else you want? My opinion of Charlie's mother was changing—and not for the better—with every one of her rude comments.

"Look. I'll ask her, but when I'm good and ready and not before." Charlie sounded like a petulant child.

"Don't be flippant. It's your duty. You must ensure the family line continues."

Charlie's voice rose several decibels. "Jesus, Mother. You're not the Queen of England."

"Just ask her." Catherine's tone left little room for argument.

Breathe. This was the first time I'd heard Charlie raise his voice. He was always Mr. Mellow. No problem. "It's cool" was his mantra. Now, this? Standing as still as the portraits in the hallway, I took a deep breath and continued to listen. That's when I heard the most amazing thing of all.

"You better ask before you run off and marry her, or else—"

Catherine's sentence was cut short by the sound of breaking glass.

"Charlie Michael Bouchard!"

Suddenly, Mac appeared in the hallway on the opposite side of the doorway carrying a tray of small sandwiches. He stopped when he saw me, assessed the situation, then nodded, before entering the sitting room. I counted to ten, then walked in. Mac was on one knee, picking up pieces of a teacup that lay broken on the coffee table with his white-gloved hands.

Catherine looked up and blushed. "Charlie can be so

clumsy sometimes."

Charlie stood staring at the floor; his arms crossed tightly.

"Accidents happen," I said, trying to lighten the mood.

The tension I was feeling had nothing to do with a broken teacup but was about the conversation that preceded it. When Charlie finally looked at me, his expression had changed. He dropped his arms and grabbed several sandwiches with his left hand and held out his right.

"Come on. We're going to find my dad. He's outside somewhere."

Catherine plastered on a serene smile as she stood ramrod straight, her toes digging into the carpet.

"Nice meeting you," I said with as much civility as I could muster before Charlie dragged me out the double French doors onto a stone patio surrounded by rose bushes in full bloom.

Once outside, he handed me two of the petite triangles. "These will hold us over until we can find some real food. Come on. Dad's down by the pond. We'll say a quick hello and then let's get out of here."

Forty-five minutes later, we were at In and Out eating Double Doubles and french fries. We'd been talking about his mother, his father, and the whole awkward mess. When I told him I wanted lots of kids, he turned a tender shade of pink.

He dropped his head. "You heard. I'm so embarrassed. Ever since Phillip died all my mother cares about is continuing the bloodline … as if we are fucking royalty or something."

"Well, you sort of are." I popped a couple of fries in my mouth.

"But that's what I like about you and what my mother liked about you—"

"Wait? She liked me?" You could have fooled me, I thought.

"Yes. She doesn't sit on her feet in front of just anyone."

"Well, that settles it then." I laughed.

Charlie ate the last of the fries before saying, "You didn't seem to care about all of the trappings of wealth. Mom liked that you didn't make a big deal about the money."

"You *told* me not to be impressed, not to care."

Charlie leaned in. "Were you impressed?"

"To be honest, it isn't my style."

Charlie beamed. "Right? It's so over the top. When we buy a house together it will be simple, hopefully near the beach."

"I'd like that. Are we going to get a cat?" I asked.

"Why would you think that?" Charlie asked before finishing off his burger.

"The portrait in the hallway."

"What?"

"In the portrait in the hallway, a cat is leaning into you. A calico."

Charlie smirked. "Oh, that cat. That is an imaginary cat. Phillip and I named him Roger. We weren't allowed real pets indoors. We had horses because rich people have horses. But no dogs, cats, birds, or fish inside the house, only people, and even then ..."

"Then why the cat in the portrait?"

"Mother thought a cat would give the painting a warm, homey feel. Having a pet in the painting portrays our family as the kind of people who love animals. My mother is not an animal person. The only time she visits the horse stables is to show off the stallions to her rich friends. She doesn't even ride. The imaginary cat was the perfect con. Unlike a dog, no one asks about a cat. They assume it's off doing its independent cat thing."

"So ... cat person or dog person?"

"Definitely a dog person, although I've never had one."

His answer made me feel warm all over as if I'd discovered everything I needed to know about the man with whom I was falling in love.

Chapter Three

Snap – Sit

I hear her stirring. I jump off the couch and trot through the open door into her sleeping room. I spring onto the bed. I settle myself in a ball. I press into the curve of her body and sigh. Her hand reaches out and scratches my head before she drapes a heavy arm over me. When I was a puppy, this was where I slept. She never left me alone. We've been together forever. She places her mouth close to my good ear. Her warm breath tickles. In a voice meant only for me, she whispers, "My Rae. My little Rae Rae."

We always start our day with a morning cuddle. The rise and fall of her chest calms and reassures me. Running my hand over her silky fur is as soothing to me as I'm guessing it is for her. I've never been with a man who understood the art of the cuddle as much as Rae. With men, if it's a cuddle before sex, the cuddle doesn't last long because as soon as I'm pressed against him, he becomes aroused. If the cuddle is after sex, the arm draped over my waist becomes increasingly heavy as he falls asleep, snoring in my ear. No. Men don't know how to cuddle like my dog.

I can't believe she is almost eighteen weeks old. She was born on Halloween, and she has bewitched me since the moment she was delivered into my outstretched arms. I find everything she does enchanting. The tilt of her head as if to say, what? The way she sits on my feet when I'm working. How she talks with rolling Rs, sighs, barks, and cries. She shows me in a hundred ways that she loves me unconditionally, which is more than I can say for the people in my life. Unlike my mother, Rae is unselfish. Unlike my father, Rae has never doubted me. And unlike my ex-husband, Rae would never hurt me. I love my dog with my whole being, which sounds like I'm a psycho, but I don't think so. Then again, most crazy people probably don't think they are psycho either. Hmmm.

My girl has always been different. Quiet. Not like other people who are loud and shout. She talks to me with her hands, small sounds, and soft whispers. When we are around other people there is so much noise. Living with my quiet girl makes me feel calm.

Our morning cuddle comes to an end when one of us can't hold it any longer. Today, it's Rae, letting me know with a single bark that she wants outside. The backyard is covered with an unbroken blanket of thin spring snow. I let Rae outside and head to the bathroom. By the time I'm finished, she is at the sliding glass door, pawing to come in. She leaps onto the bed before I can stop her. Rae's paws are wet, and she has small pompoms of snow clinging to the fur on her legs. Oh well, it's only water.

I sit on the edge of the bed, Rae at my side, and take in the beauty of my little piece of paradise. The sun has broken through what's left of the storm clouds, turning the small icicles hanging from the roof's eave into chandelier crystals. A shaft of light slants through the sliding glass door and casts a spotlight on my bird paintings.

I stand and reverently touch each bird before leaving the bedroom. Walking through the house, Rae following at my heels, I water all my plants. I have a braided Benjamina Ficus tree that sits in the corner of the living room. I have to use a stepladder to reach the six Pothos plants that line the top of the kitchen cabinets, their long strings of leaves running the length of the cabinets. The Aloe Vera, a collection of succulents in colorful pots, and my plant rescues are the last to be watered. When I left my home in Laguna Beach, the only things I took were clothing, the two bird paintings, and all of these plants.

After my morning yoga or should I say *doga*—since Rae has to get in on the action by jumping on my lap whenever I'm seated, walking under me during cat and cow stretches, licking my face during downward dog—I sip my tea, pay a few bills online, and I discover that my monthly stipend has been deposited. As the new garden steward for the community garden, I receive a small salary April through October, courtesy of Berta's bequeathment to the garden. Between my newsletter gigs and this small salary, I'm doing okay. I'm even setting money aside each month, although not a lot. My goal is to buy a small cabin of my own. I've come to think of Pine City as my home. With Frank here, a friend, and of course, Rae, I'm feeling happy and content for the first time in years.

Thirty minutes later, Rae and I are on our way to meet Frank at the garden. The spring snow has already melted, leaving the streets clear and wet. We arrive an hour before orientation to help set up and to let Rae do her thing ... chase rabbits. As we turn left, Rae pops up, nose pressed against the window. She knows where we are and what is about to happen. She lets out an excited *woof.*

Rabbits. Rabbits. Rabbits. This is the place with all the rabbits. Come on. Come on. Let me out.

As I pull up and park, Frank climbs out of his car and walks over. "Morning."

I smile and wave. To look at Frank and me, you'd never suspect we were father and daughter, especially now with my jet-black hair. At six foot four, Frank is a good eleven inches taller. When he hugs me, which he never does in public, I fit neatly under his arm. We have the same hazel eyes and the same cowlick that flips our hair over our right eye. According to Mom, Frank's hair used to be a deep, chocolate brown. Now it's salt and pepper, leaning more toward salt. Frank teases me that the whole Berta thing aged him a good ten years.

"Is Rabbit Slayer ready to go to work?"

I point to the passenger window where Rae is pawing at the glass.

"May I?" Frank asks.

I nod and Frank opens the car door, being careful not to be in the line of fire of the furry cannonball. Rae shoots out of the car and races to the garden gate where she dances in circles of anticipation. Frank walks over and talks to her as he twirls the numbers on the combination lock.

"Ready to chase some rabbits and send them running?"

Rae was born ready. When the gate swings open, Rae charges ahead until the first smell stops her like she's run into a wall. Nose to the dirt, she begins tracking.

So many smells. So many wonderful smells. A rabbit was here. A squirrel ran across the dirt and up into one of the wooden boxes that smells of rotting plants. It's gone now. A lizard. Mice. Lots of mice. A rabbit left a pile of fresh treats. I try one. Not bad. I eat a few more then move on. The scent grows stronger as I move closer to the little house. A rabbit darts out from behind a wooden box. Something clicks inside of me and I'm off, chasing down that rabbit until it squeezes through a hole under the fence. Woof. Woof. Woof. The man everyone calls Frank rushes up.

"Good girl," he says, pulling a meaty treat from his pocket.

He snaps his fingers and I sit. Then he gives me the treat. He likes these treats, too, and together we eat. My girl joins us.

"The rabbits have dug a hole under the fence. I'm going to

mark the spot so I can fix it later. Maybe the Rabbit Slayer will find another. Where there is one rabbit, there are bound to be more," Frank says.

Nodding, I head to the shed where the table and chairs are kept. I don't like that Frank calls Rae the Rabbit Slayer. Rae has never actually caught and killed a rabbit. She's fast, but not that fast. But since I haven't told my father Rae's name, he's allowed to call her whatever he wants, just like everyone else. Rae doesn't recognize Rabbit Slayer as her name, so I let it go.

As I'm spinning the combination lock, Rae rushes by in a blur of black and white and I hear Frank yell with glee, "She's onto another one." I don't know who is having more fun, my dog, or my father.

Opening the shed door, I freeze as the memory of what happened here greets me like a boxer's jab. Berta Johnson found dead in the shed. Dead in the shed. The unintended rhyme makes me shudder. I was the last person to see her alive. I take a step backward as I remember the moment. Berta screaming at me about Frank choosing me over her as his assistant. Me storming out. Frank witnessing my distraught exit, then finding Berta, and believing I had killed her.

Looking to the right at the bare dirt next to the fence where the compost pile used to be, my stomach does a flip-flop. Frank had buried Berta in the compost pile to protect his daughter from going to jail. At that point, I had no idea he was my dad. I am still amazed that he did that ... risked going to jail for a daughter he barely knew.

Frank ended up spending a couple of hours in jail until his wife Sylvia could post bail. At the hearing, Frank pleaded guilty to concealing an accidental death, which is a misdemeanor … even though at the time, he thought I had killed Berta. He was fined $3,000 and 30 hours of community service, which working in the community garden would satisfy. Judge Senft, who belonged to the same bike club as Frank, had told him with a chuckle, that the next time he found a dead body he should call the sheriff instead of taking matters into his own hands.

While I never liked Berta—most people didn't—I certainly would not have killed her. She was a bossy, know-it-all who thought that because I couldn't speak, she needed to shout when she talked to me. Who could have guessed that her accidental death would bring about so much change for so many people, especially for me?

The biggest change? I discovered my father hadn't died in Vietnam as my mother had told me. That was a two-prong revelation—I had a father and my mother had lied to me my entire life. I'm still wrapping my mind around that deception.

Then there was the money. Apparently, Berta had money. Lots and lots of money. She had set up an endowment or some such thing that now subsidizes the plot fees that used to pay for maintenance and now provides the garden steward—me—with a small salary. I'm guessing she's rolling over in her grave knowing I'm the garden steward. She didn't think I was even qualified to be the assistant let alone the head honcho, even though I have dual degrees in horticulture and nutrition.

Securing both shed doors open with latches, I step into the cool interior. The chairs are leaning against the wall and the table is buried behind them. I hope Frank will come help but then I hear Rae barking over by the orchard and a triumphant whoop from Frank.

"She's found another one!"

Guess I'm doing this myself.

Forty-five minutes later, we are ready for orientation. Since I can't talk, Frank, who is officially now the "garden assistant," will do the presentation. My job is to hand out the liability forms and keep track of who wants which bed. Then I'll follow up with the people who didn't show up at this first orientation via email or text.

Based on the emails so far, no one is interested in taking over Berta's raised bed, just like last year. So as not to waste the bed, I will grow Berta's heirloom tomatoes again. I find it funny that no one wanted Berta's bed, but no one had a problem eating the delicious tomatoes I grew there. A solid case of the Little Red Hen, a story I heard when growing up in the commune to encourage all the kids to participate in the growing of food. The moral of the story … if you don't help grow the food, you don't get to eat the food, something the gardeners at the Community Garden have not grasped.

The compost piles had to be moved to a new location

because knowing that Berta had been buried under one of them gave some of the gardeners the willies. That first season, we did lose a half dozen gardeners. But now new gardeners have arrived who either don't know or don't care about what happened, including Judge Senft's wife.

Glancing again at where the piles used to be and then at Frank, I'm still amazed and a bit confused that a man would go to such lengths to protect a daughter he barely knew. I'm sad when I remember all my fatherless years. Frank is more than sad … sometimes he's downright angry. He has no problem letting my mother know how he feels about being cheated out of being a parent. Frank would have been a terrific father had my mother bothered telling him I'd been born.

Rae and I stand several feet inside the gate to greet people. I wave and smile as I hand out liability forms. Rae wags her tail and goes up to the people she knows for head scratches and praise. The Woo sisters, identical twins that no one can tell apart, including me, show up in their gardening outfits of white long-sleeved shirts, black slacks, and colorful tennis shoes. Rae immediately runs up to Ling. Or is it, Chen? Rae knows who's who.

Good smells. I hope she remembers. She snaps. I sit, my tail wagging, clearing away the wet dirt behind me. She bends at the waist and extends her hand to me. I lift my paw and place it in her hand.

"Good to see you again, Princess."

She stands. Her hand disappears into the opening in her pants. My nose twitches. Banana, peanut butter, blueberries, and oats. She remembered. She pulls the cookie out of hiding at last. Once the cookie is in my mouth, I race away. I wait until I am under the table to eat my treat.

I smile and make the sign for "thank you." The sisters smile back.

"Ling loves making healthy dog treats. Besides the blueberry treat, she also makes one lamb and a variety of veggies. We sell both at our shop in the Village if you ever want more. Your dog loves them."

Ahh. This must be Chen. I nod and mouth the word okay while making the okay sign. As Ling walks to the chairs, Rae shows up for a second treat. I watch as Ling snaps her fingers and Rae sits. Then Ling uses the sign for 'all gone,' which I taught her last year so she wouldn't be hounded by Rae. With her left palm open, facing up, and horizontal to the ground, she sweeps her open right palm across her left hand and then closes it into a fist. Rae lifts her paw for a shake, but Ling repeats the sign. Rae gives up on receiving a second treat and rejoins me near the entrance, flopping down at my feet in doggie disappointment.

Chen stands next to me as the other gardeners arrive. Since they don't know whether she is Chen or Ling, they say a general "Hi" to both of us as they take the forms from my hand.

Chen shakes her head. "People still can't tell us apart, but your dog knows."

I make the sign for "morning," which is what Chen's name means in Chinese—right arm bent at the elbow, extends out from the body with palm open and facing up. I move my hand and arm from horizontal to vertical.

Chen smiles and imitates the sign saying, "Morning. Yes. I remember the sign."

Then changing the subject, Chen continues. "Ling will have everything you need for the newsletter ready by the end of the week. Do you think that is enough time to have it go out by May first?"

Sure, I mouth as I nod.

"Great. I'll let her know. I'm going to tell her you need everything by Thursday. That way you'll have it by Friday. She needs deadlines."

I know what she means. I currently write three newsletters. One for the community garden, which is part of my job description as the garden steward including all social media. One for Ling and Chen's apothecary shop in the Village, and one for the nursery where I used to work. I write most of the short articles for the community garden and the nursery newsletters, except for a small Tips & Tricks column by Frank and input on monthly sales from the nursery. But the apothecary newsletter is ninety percent Ling, which means part of what I'm being paid for is bugging Ling to send me her copy.

Suddenly, Rae is on her feet, tail wagging.

Woof. Woof. Here comes another person, I know. I like her

when I see her here, but not at the other place. At the other place, she wears a white coat and smells like a dozen different kinds of animals ... dogs, cats, lizards, and birds. In the small room, she looks into my mouth. She uses her fingers to open my eyes wide. She lifts my ears to peer inside. Sometimes she pricks me with a pointy thing that has a sharp smell that I don't like. Here she smells good. I can still smell the other animals, but the smell is weaker here. There is no white coat. I'm safe. Sometimes she has treats. They are not as good as the other ones. They are hard. The smells are not as strong. She hugs my girl. She looks down at me.

"Look who's here. It's my favorite doodle. Are you a good girl?"

She comes down to my level on one knee. Woof. She snaps her fingers and I sit. I know what's coming. I place my paw on her knee.

"She hasn't forgotten me."

The woman laughs. Her hand disappears inside her pants. When it comes out there is a treat. I gently pull the treat from her fingers. I run to the shelter of the table.

"I loved your April first newsletter. So much good advice," says Dr. Barb as she brushes the dirt off her knee.

I make the sign for thanks.

"I was thinking. Maybe I should have a newsletter for the practice. Short articles and helpful tips. I like how you included a recipe. I could have recipes for healthy dog treats."

I'm smiling and nodding as I'm thinking about how I'm

going to manage another newsletter. The extra money could go directly into savings, helping me reach my goal sooner than later. How many newsletters per year? I mouth, but she doesn't understand. I use my fingers, showing her six, then ten, then twelve. Her face lights up when she understands what I'm asking her.

"I'm thinking of starting with six times a year and then measuring the response. I can use the newsletter to highlight specials and remind people of seasonal issues like rattlesnake training before summer starts. Things like that."

While she is talking, I hand out a few more forms.

"Sorry. This isn't the best time to talk about this, is it? I was just so excited imagining all the different articles and ideas that I couldn't wait to talk to you."

My okay sign lets Dr. Barb know it's no big deal. My smile transforms from happy to sad as Rose and her two granddaughters, ages seven and five, come through the gate.

"Hi, Lizzy," the girls say in unison. "Is your dog here?"

I point in the direction of the table and chairs, and the girls go running off, Rose walking slowly with her cane after them. A deep sadness comes over me as I watch the girls race to the table. How long will I feel this way whenever I'm around small children?

"Maybe we can talk about the newsletter later," says Dr. Barb, sounding disappointed.

Turning back to Dr. Barb, I make the sign for "sorry." I take out my phone and text her. "Do you want to meet and go over details … say Sunday morning? I can pull together a few different templates to start."

The smile returns to her face. "That sounds great. What time and where?"

Texting her the address to Keri's Place, I suggest ten o'clock.

After she reads my text she says, "Great. See you Sunday," before heading to the chairs.

Dr. Barb was the one who figured out that Rae has a deformed eardrum and is mostly deaf in her right ear. Dr. Barb said that I was the perfect person for my dog since I can't talk anyway. Deaf and dumb, I thought.
The last person to arrive is Abby. She hugs me and together we head to the chairs where Frank had already started his presentation.

The front door is barely open before Rae races inside, sending the pile of mail delivered through the mail slot into disarray. I collect the assortment of envelopes, catalogs, and junk mail and notice a pink envelope decorated with Easter eggs. Mom.

Mom has a thing about sending cards, real cards, addressed by hand and delivered by snail mail. The stamp usually matches the occasion, and this card is no exception with its Forever stamp featuring red, white, and yellow tulips. She told me she buys the cards in bulk but the stamps she picks out one at a time. Ever since I moved away, she started sending cards to keep in touch. Birthday? Of course. Valentine's Day? Sure. Memorial Day,

Fourth of July, maybe. I even receive a card on Veterans' Day, which is weird since I'm not a veteran. Charlie used to get a kick out of my mom's cards.

I take the mail into the kitchen where I sort through everything as I stand, dropping the junk mail and catalogs into my circular filing bin. I save the pink envelope for last, flipping it over I read Happy Easter. On the inside, it says, Love Mom. No note this time. It's just a silly card with a rabbit but Mom will expect a thank you call or text. Pulling out my phone I discover five missed calls and a text message, all from Mom. The text message says, "Call me, NOW!"

My mouth goes dry. Something is wrong. Why didn't I hear my phone ring? Oh, that's right. I silenced my phone during the orientation. According to the time stamp, all of her calls came in while I was driving home. Five missed calls and five voicemails. I tap the voicemail icon and wait with dread. My mother's high-pitched voice fills the kitchen with a blast of staccato sentences that makes my heart race and has me reaching for the edge of the kitchen counter to steady myself.

"He's here. At the front door. Charlie is here. Out of the nuthouse. Banging on the front door. Standing on my front porch. What should I do? Call me."

This is it … the moment I've been dreading. Rae barks sharply, scaring me so badly that my phone flies out of my hands and lands with a thud on the kitchen floor. With shaky hands, I retrieve my phone and call Mom.

Chapter Four

Five Years Ago – May

"You look like an angel," my mother said as she entered the garden room that had been converted into my bridal suite.

Standing in front of the ornate free-standing mirror, I had to admit I loved how I looked. Catherine would have been mortified if she knew I'd bought my simple dress online for under two hundred dollars. The champagne color was more flattering to my pale complexion and dark hair than a white dress would have been. The V-neckline showed off a discreet amount of cleavage, which Charlie had approved of immediately. I'd broken tradition by letting my fiancé help me pick my dress.

My sleeveless, chiffon, midi dress had lace at the shoulders and down the back. It was one of the few things I'd been allowed to choose for my wedding. Allowed is probably not accurate. Charlie and I had to fight for the right to choose what we'd wear including my dress, hairstyle, and jewelry, much to my soon-to-be mother-in-law's consternation. If she'd had her way, I'd look like a fancy cake topper with a full organza skirt, a mile-long train, glass slippers, and my hair in some sort of updo bejeweled with diamonds. I might be exaggerating a bit, but not by much.

Mom had picked up two crystal flutes of champagne off the silver tray on the coffee table before joining me in front of the mirror. She handed me a glass, lifting hers in a toast.

"Here's to the new princess of Orange County. Someday all this could be yours," she said in awe as she looked around the room.

I took a healthy sip of champagne, the bubbles tickling my nose. "Not really. They made me sign a prenup."

Mom looked shocked. "But you're entitled to something, right?"

"Maybe, but it will depend on how long we've been married and how many children I 'produce.'" I said it lightly, but inside I was screaming. The whole thing about 'producing children' made it sound like I was nothing more than a baby factory. I'd objected, for all the good it did. Catherine was not going to budge on that one … no signature, no marriage. I did love Charlie and I did want kids, so I signed their ridiculous document.

"Well, that's okay, then. As long as you come away with something. They are just protecting their wealth. You know how rich people are. But I'm glad you'll be taken care of in the end. Boy, this champagne is good. I'm having another glass.

Want one?"

"No thanks." The fact that I had to produce children to be awarded more money in the event of a divorce didn't faze Mom in the least, as long as I was going to come away with 'something in the deal.'

Moving to the settee, the same settee where Charlie and I had sat the first time I met Catherine, I found it as uncomfortable as ever. I finished my champagne and set the flute on the silver tray. Changing my mind, I took another.

"Good for you. This stuff probably cost hundreds of dollars per bottle," my mom said, plopping down next to me and picking up another flute, her third but who's counting. She looked down at my bare feet with my toenails painted pale pink with a rhinestone on each of my big toes.

"What kind of shoes are you going to wear?"

"We're going barefoot," I said, nodding in satisfaction. Another small battle we'd won.

Charlie and I had both talked about a small beach wedding. He'd even wanted to be married in the ocean sitting astride matching surfboards, but I'd nixed that idea. A beach wedding, however, did sound perfect. The first thing we did was go online and buy this dress and a pair of champagne linen pants with a matching short-sleeved button shirt for Charlie. When his mother found out what we'd done she about lost her mind. I let Charlie fight that battle and for once he won. Unfortunately, the price of his victory was exorbitant … we won the battle but lost the war.

Catherine would control everything else about the wedding and reception, from the location (the estate backyard) to the flowers (lilies, lilies, lilies), from the guest list (mostly her people) to the cake (a ten-tiered monstrosity). Charlie and I were each allowed twenty friends out of the three hundred and fifty who were invited. Charlie and I had a huge fight the night he told me what he had to give up so I could wear what I wanted.

"Babe. You get to the dress you picked out. You should be happy. Who cares about the rest? It's just another opportunity for Mother to show off the house and gardens to all her rich friends. We are simply an excuse for a huge party," Charlie said.

"But it's my wedding. I should have a say in what kind of cake I want."

Charlie shrugged. "It's just a cake. Who the hell cares? I've never understood why women care so much about wedding stuff. It's a total waste of money. It's over in a day and all you have left are pictures. Stop fighting her. Mother always has her way in the end. Besides, she's paying for everything. It's her money she's wasting, and she has plenty of it, so who cares."

I was silent. This was not what I'd pictured when I thought of my wedding day.

Charlie had sat next to me and taken my hands in his. When I didn't look at him but stared at our hands, he pulled one hand away and used it to gently turn my face to look at him.

"Look. I don't care about this damn wedding or the reception or any of it. I just want to be married to you and start our life together. You'll throw the bouquet. We'll cut some cake, drink expensive-ass champagne, and dance until it's time to board the plane and leave it all behind. Five hours later, we'll be lying on a beach in Hawaii. Now that's what sounds good to me."

Reluctantly I had agreed.

It was time. Mom played with the flowers that had been braided into my hair and adjusted the single strand of pearls that was my something borrowed from Catherine. The wedding coordinator handed me my bouquet … four dozen champagne roses that cascaded down to my knees. The bouquet felt like it weighed a ton. Mom, in her peach, floor-length gown, which probably cost more than my dress, was walking me down the aisle. The music sounded, the double doors opened with a flourish, and we stepped out onto … sand? Fine, white silica sand crept between my toes. My eyes followed the path of sand directly to the flower-covered arbor where Charlie and a preacher wearing a Hawaiian shirt waited.

Mom was having a difficult time walking up the aisle in her heels, so about halfway to the arbor, she stopped and kicked off her shoes. With over three hundred people in attendance, the aisle was half the length of a football field, with rows and rows of chairs on either side. There was no bride's side or groom's side, and I had no family seated in the front row. My mother was my only family. We'd opted for no bridesmaids or groomsmen, which Catherine surprisingly agreed to. My guess…more attention for her son, the fabulous surroundings, and of course, herself.

As I walked down the aisle, I locked eyes with Charlie. There was a string of energy that connected us, growing stronger and stronger the closer I came. With three feet to go, he stretched out his hand to me. It was such a simple gesture, but it made me tingle all over. We stood facing each other, our toes wriggling deeper into the sand, eyes locked on each other. Words were said, promises were made, sealed by a long, deep kiss, that I'm sure had Catherine cringing, then we headed back down the aisle and were escorted to the lower garden for photos. Forty-five minutes later, we joined the party. We entered the tented reception area to the cheers of the assembled mass like we were conquering heroes returning from some distant battle.

During the required dancing with the parents, Mr. Bouchard put his mouth next to my ear and asked, "How did you like the sand?"

"I loved it. I was surprised, though, since the last I had heard, it was to be a red runner."

Mr. Bouchard nodded.

"That was me," he said with obvious delight. "I had a ton of sand delivered from one of my golf courses while Catherine was away. By the time she came back, the crew had created the aisle and the area under the gazebo. What could she do?"

"I bet she was furious."

"Yes, but she never let on. I'll pay for it later, but it was worth it. I knew Charlie wanted a beach wedding and this was the best I could do."

I stood on my tippy toes and kissed my new father-in-law on the cheek.

"It was perfect. I hope your punishment isn't too harsh."

He shrugged. "I've done worse," he said with a wicked grin I hadn't seen before.

Then he twirled me around, handing me off to one of Charlie's friends. And so, the evening went, a swirling, whirlwind of activities ... dancing, drinking, eating, being introduced to dozens of "important" people. Before I knew it, we were climbing into the back of the limo to be driven to the airport, my mom standing next to Catherine, both of them with tears in their eyes.

Hawaii was sheer perfection. Warm tropical breezes kissed our naked bodies as we lay in bed each morning and listened to the waves crash on the shore. With all the lovemaking, sometimes in the morning, but usually after Charlie came back from surfing, and always at night, I was ravenous. I devoured our daily breakfast of fresh mango, papayas, pineapple, and croissants. Then I didn't even have to leave my lounge chair on the beach as lunch was delivered in a wicker basket by our butler. Dinner was usually at sunset, on the sand served by the light of tiki torches, at a table for two complete with white linens and never-ending champagne. I gained five pounds and was surprised it wasn't more. Even the weather cooperated as did the waves, which made Charlie the happiest I'd seen him since the start of the wedding planning. On one of the calmer days, he even attempted to teach me to surf on a longboard. Even though he was a patient teacher … epic fail. But I had fun trying.

On our last night, we sat holding hands across the white tablecloth, waves crashing, tiki light flickering, and champagne making us warm and fuzzy.

"Babe. This has been the best seven days of my life," Charlie said, squeezing my hand. "I never want to leave."

"Me, too," I said, and meant it.

Then he cocked his head and gave me a sheepish grin. "And maybe, with all the sex, we made a baby?"

Something about the way he said it, took the sparkle off the moment as the whole "produce an heir" thing came crashing back like waves pounding the shore. Was that what our lovemaking was all about? Making a baby? I shook my head to dispel the thought. That was his mother talking. Charlie wasn't like that.

Chapter Five

Point – Lie Down

My stomach is twisted into knots, making my morning tea taste bitter. Sitting at the dining room table, Rae at my feet, my laptop open and waiting, I'm supposed to be working on Dr. Barb's newsletter. Instead, I'm staring at the screen, zoned out. I feel like that woman in the television commercial … the one who holds a happy face on a stick in front of her face to hide her depression. Only I'm not hiding depression. I'm hiding fear. Ever since I talked to Mom, I've been obsessing over Charlie's release from the hospital. I've always known this day would come, but it was easy to forget once I began feeling at home in Pine City.

Charlie had been sentenced to four years at the state mental hospital instead of prison with a re-evaluation at the end of his term. It's only been two and a half years. I thought I'd have more time. I'd pushed any thought of Charlie's return into the fog of "the future." Now the fog has cleared, the future is now, and Charlie is a free man, free to find his ex-wife as he promised on the day they sent him away.

I don't know how he will do it, but I'm certain he will. He doesn't know I have a father, a father in Pine City, meaning he has no reason to look here. The only person from my former life who knows where I am is my mother and she would never tell him. Never. So why am I walking on pins and needles, glancing over my shoulder, jumping at shadows?

Charlie doesn't have any connections with the police or ways to track my car. He's not a hacker who can find me through DMV records like in the movies. But the one thing he does have is money. Lots of money. I bet it was his family's money that garnered his early release. Now money will buy him information, or maybe he'll hire a private detective to track me down ... more his style. Why break a sweat when you can hire someone else to do your dirty work? My knee starts jumping. Rae whines.

Something is wrong. Lizzy is not herself. She smells different. I lay my head on her vibrating leg. She scratches my head. Her mind is somewhere else. I am not comforted or reassured. I whine again. She rubs behind my ears. I need to move outside. Outside is better. I run to the door and bark. I look back at her. Will she come? She is not moving. I bark again. Here she comes. We go outside. She sits on a chair and stares. I find my throwing disc and drop it at her feet. She picks it up and tosses it.

Good. She's doing something. I bring it back but don't let go. I tug and pull. She holds steady. I swing my head back and forth. She lets me win. I drop my toy. She throws it again. I can tell she is not paying attention. I lie down across her feet, my head on my paws. I don't know what else I can do.

Sitting outside, I force myself to inhale deeply. The scent of pine dances on a light breeze. A pinecone drops with a plunk into the yard and sends Rae over to investigate. A mountain chickadee calls its high-pitched name from a tree branch. Rae cocks her head to listen. Chickadee-dee-dee. Rae barks once in reply. Normally this would make me smile, but not today. It feels like I'm standing blindfolded in the middle of the street knowing eventually a car is going to hit me. I feel jumpy … powerless.

Powerless. That's the word. It's more than fear. It's the feeling that when he finds me there will be nothing I can do should he go off the rails again. Off the rails … the perfect description of his "episode" as his mother called it. Charlie and I would be chugging along, riding the train of our marriage, complete with the normal ups and downs, and then bam, train wreck. His lawyer had a name for it, "Intermittent Explosive Disorder." A fancy name for losing your shit.

I walk back inside, shaking my head. Rae follows, looking as forlorn as I feel. How can I protect myself? As if my phone can read my thoughts, it pings. Rae runs to the front door, confused by the sound and where it's coming from. I look at the screen. It's a text from Mom. Charlie has stopped by again. I flinch as if I've been stung. Rae reacts by barking. I'm making her nervous as well. The first time Charlie showed up, Mom didn't open the door, but that hadn't stopped Charlie. He stood on the front porch and talked and talked. He wouldn't leave until my mom threatened to call the police. Now he's back again?

I read her text. "Charlie came by again. This time he left a bouquet. It's quite lovely. Over a dozen champagne roses, just like your wedding bouquet. And a card. I'll take a picture of the flowers. Do you want me to open the card? Let me know."

I feel like growling like Rae when I read Mom's text. Charlie is trying to win Mom over. "Quite lovely" indeed. Mom is a pushover for male attention, expensive gifts, and most of all flowers. Of course, Charlie knows this. I wish I had more faith in Mom's ability to resist his charms, but I don't.

Pacing back and forth in the living room, Rae tries to keep up. Rae is a natural herding dog and as such, prefers to walk behind me, sometimes nudging me with her nose. But this pacing has her confused. I keep changing direction, making it difficult for her to stay behind.

I'm not sure what we are doing. First, we walk to the wall, then we walk to the table. Wall, table. Wall, table. My girl is making me nervous. I stop in the middle of the room and sit. I whine. She stops. Kneeling beside me she whispers words, lots of words, into my ear. I can tell by her tone that she is sad. I lick her face. I hope that helps.

This is ridiculous. I'm asking my dog what I should do.

How can I be prepared when Charlie shows up at my door? I'll ask
him to go away. I'll call the police. But what if he goes ballistic?
It's like he's not himself. All full of rage. He's a full seven inches
taller and outweighs me by at least sixty pounds. He's strong.
I used to describe his body as "ripped." His arms and upper body
have been shaped by years of surfing. They probably let him surf
at the mental hospital, after all, it is in Malibu.

Maybe I should buy a gun. Could I shoot him? I don't think
so. A taser? But what if he catches me with my taser tucked inside
my pack or when I'm in the house? Am I going to walk around
with a taser in my back pocket? I don't think so. My mind is
running around in circles grasping at anything and everything. Rae
cries and licks my face again. I give her head a reassuring rub
before standing.

I stand in the middle of my living room, Rae sitting at my
feet looking up at me expectantly as I try to find answers. How can
a smaller person defend against someone physically larger? There
must be something. I move to the dining room table, turn on my
computer, and sit. I search for "best self-defense for women."

I spent the next hour reading about all the different types
of self-defense programs … their pros and cons, and which ones
would work best for my situation. Doing something makes me feel
better. I'm being proactive and that helps relax me. I'm not
interested in fighting or competing or defending against a gun or a
knife or even multiple attackers. It's pretty simple. It's no mystery
who my attacker will be.

I've narrowed it down to Krav Maga, Taekwondo, and Gracie Jiu-Jitsu. Next, I look up what's available here on the mountain. No one teaches Krav Maga but there is a Taekwondo and a Jiu-Jitsu Academy. Taekwondo focuses on kicking. Me kicking Charlie with my short little legs? What a joke. I might land one good kick before he'd grab my leg and toss me in the air like a ragdoll. Jiu-Jitsu is the winner.

What sells me on Jiu-Jitsu is the school has a class for women called, "Women Empowered" that focuses on defensive maneuvers. A short video on the site shows a small woman, smaller than me, being strangled by a larger, taller male. When the man's hands encircle her throat, my body freezes. My heart races. My lungs contract. A cold sweat prickles my forehead and the top of my lip. It is as if I am transported back to that awful day. But then the woman breaks free! I watch the video again and again. Could it be this easy? Then I feel something I haven't felt in a long time … hope.

It's 6 pm on a Wednesday and I'm sitting in my car outside the Pine City Jiu-Jitsu Academy. I watch as women—tall, short, athletic, out-of-shape, older, and younger—walk across the parking lot and enter through a glass door. It's a popular class and I am relieved. I was worried there would only be a few women, which would have put the spotlight on me, the new gal who can't speak. Now, I'll be one of about seven or eight and will hopefully blend in. After a bout of indecision, I clip the leash on Rae before walking to the door and heading inside.

From the outside, the building looks like a two-story warehouse with steel siding and no windows. As I step inside, undertones of sweat and bleach tickle my nostrils as I pause to look around. My first impression is a giant boxing ring without ropes. The walls on two sides are lined with six-foot-tall mats. The third wall is set back about four feet from the mat. A hallway disappears down the middle leading to who knows where. On the left of the hallway is a large shoe cubby where the women are storing their shoes and water bottles. On the right, is a closed door and a large picture window that reveals an office with a man seated at a desk. I find a bench against the fourth wall that is also set back from the mat and have a seat. I point my finger down and Rae reluctantly lies at my feet. I'm sure if I took her off the leash, she'd have a ball running around discovering new smells. Rae is all about the nose.

This place is full of good smells. I want to walk around. But my girl is nervous. She needs me, so I sit on her feet, put my nose in the air, and take in the delicious odors. Smells are coming off the women ... perfume, coconut shampoo, sweat, and lavender lotion. I pick up the scents that stick to their clothes ... dogs, cats, a bird. Someone has a bird? Weird. I didn't know people let birds sit on them. She doesn't know it, but the bird pooped on her shoulder. The women are taking off their shoes and there is an explosion of new smells in the air, not all of them good. I like this place.

While there are no trophy cabinets, there are colorful

championship banners mounted high on the wall on either side of a painted logo—a black ring around a white circle. Inside the ring, in white letters across the top, it says, "Team Tanaka Pierce" and curving up on the bottom, "Pine City Jiu-Jitsu Academy." In the center of the white circle is the outline of a black triangle with the right leg of the triangle bent into the middle near the top. I have no idea what it means, but it looks like a mountain to me. I sit back against the wall and watch as the women greet each other before bowing slightly and stepping barefoot onto the mat.

My ears perk up when I hear a door open. I look around. A man who smells very different from the women walks out. Behind him, a dog. The dog sees me and trots my way. I stand, ready. My girl holds my leash a bit tighter. She is ready as well. The dog is a boy. He approaches slowly. His tail is wagging. He is bigger and older than I am. We sniff noses. Then circle round to sniff butts. Then he walks off to join his man. That was boring. I'm about to lie down when my girl stands, and we follow the dog to his man.

He must be the instructor. Taller than most of the women here—I'd guess almost six feet—he's wearing baggy sweatpants and a loose T-shirt imprinted with the academy logo on his broad back. Tablet in hand, I wait for him to finish speaking with one of his students. When she leaves, I take a couple of steps closer as he turns to me.

"Hi. I'm Luca. Are you interested in signing up for a class?"

For a moment, I am transfixed. His voice reminds me of a

DJ on a cool Jazz station, deep, rich, and masculine. His smile is open and friendly, and his honey-brown eyes—the same color as Rae's—never leave my face. Rae lifts and drags her paw across my leg, jolting me back to reality. I hand him my tablet so he can read what I've already typed.

"Hi. My name is Lizzy. Would it be okay if I watched a class?"

Luca looks up. "Sure. You and your dog can sit over there. If you need the restroom, it's down the hall. The drinking fountain and a dog bowl with water are outside the restroom. That's Champ," he says, pointing at the German Shepherd mix who had just introduced himself to Rae.

He bends down and rubs Rae's head saying, "He might look tough, but he's a pushover for a pretty face." Then he hands back the tablet and looks at the large school clock on the far wall. "Time to start. We can talk after class, and I can answer any questions you might have."

I nod and give him a thumbs-up before returning to the bench to regain my composure. Rae looks up at me and tilts her head as if to say, "What was that all about?" My pulse quickened, and if I could have spoken it would have been gibberish. Get a grip. I look out at all the women smiling at Luca and have new insight into why the class is full.

He reminds me of my movie star crush, Jason Momoa, the actor who played Aquaman. Both Jason and Luca have the same caramel candy complexion and exotic features. Unlike Aquaman,

Luca has his shiny black hair pulled into a sloppy man bun at the back of his head instead of cascading around his shoulders. Shaking my head, I try to dispel images of the man topless, sporting exotic tats, and holding a trident.

Rae places her paw on my knee. She knows something is up. Rubbing behind her ears I try to reassure her but she's not buying it. She moves in closer until she is leaning against my leg. If she could, she'd climb onto my lap, wrap her paws around me and yell, mine, mine, mine. She doesn't have anything to worry about. I point to the ground and Rae reluctantly lies down. I'm here to learn self-defense, not find a boyfriend. And with that in mind, I concentrate on what they are doing on the mat.

What I like so far is that everyone is dressed in comfortable street clothes, not the traditional white Gi I read about. This class is more informal, with the students calling Luca "Coach," not Sensei. Aside from the bow, everyone does before stepping onto the padded mat that fills the room, nothing screams martial arts, which I like. I'm not interested in earning colored belts, fighting in competitions, or becoming the next Karate Kid. I just want to defend myself.

The women line up with Luca at the front. He leads them through a series of warm-up stretches. I use this time to type what I want to ask him after the class. With the stretching over, the women retreat to the far wall except for a petite blonde woman who joins Luca in the center of the mat.

"Today, we are going to learn how to break away when

someone grabs you by the arm. Remember the goal is to disengage from the person and then run or walk away. We are not here to learn how to stay and fight. If you are interested in fighting, then you can join one of our other classes, but because you are here, we are learning how to react to specific situations."

The women nod in agreement.

"Because every situation can be slightly different—you could be indoors or outdoors, he could be trying to drag you into a car or a room—we are going to learn several defensive maneuvers. Annette and I will demonstrate the first maneuver, then we'll break into pairs to practice before we move on to the second and third. For the last fifteen minutes of class, we will practice what we learned last Tuesday. Any questions?" Luca looks around and finding no raised hands, begins.

As Annette faces off with Luca, I am reminded of David and Goliath. She's even shorter than I am. I am highly skeptical. How will this little thing escape? But it happens. With a couple of fluid movements, she breaks free of his grasp. I'm fascinated by the ease of the technique and how effective it is at breaking the grip.

Annette frees her wrist again and again by moving her arm through the weakest area in Luca's grip, the opening between the thumb and fingers. I watch as she bends her elbow, moving her hand towards her shoulder and her elbow towards Luca. When the other women begin practicing the move, I hear one woman say, "Hold me as tight as you can."

I watch as the woman still breaks free.

Luca and Annette are now walking around the pairs of women, adjusting their techniques. The woman who wanted her partner to hold her tighter asks Luca to hold her as tight as he can. It's a total mismatch, similar to Charlie and myself. The woman is a petite little thing and yet she breaks free. A huge smile spreads across her face and I find myself smiling as well. It can be done.

They learn how to break a two-handed grip by reaching over and through the guy's arms, grabbing their hand, and pulling their arm toward themselves while pushing their elbow toward the attacker. Not even Luca can maintain his grip on Annette when she performs the action. They demonstrate in slow motion first, talking through the technique, then at full speed. I gasp in amazement at how effective the move is and hope no one heard me.

"If you do this move fast enough, and thrust your elbow up, there is a good chance you will pop the guy under his chin with your elbow, which wouldn't be a bad thing …"

One of the women yells, "Damn straight."

"Remember, a victory is arriving home safe. Seventy-eight percent of the time, your assailant is someone you know."

You got that right.

"Part of what you are learning is how to scale your actions to the situation. For example, you are alone, walking through the Village, and some guy grabs you by the arm and starts harassing you."

Luca turns to Annette and grabs her arm, then acting drunk

and surly he says, "Hey, sweet thing. How about you come home with me for some fun."

Luca turns back to the women. "This guy is obviously an asshole with bad intentions. Go ahead and break his hold aggressively, and pop that elbow up with force as you step toward him. If you clip him hard under his chin in the process, so be it. But be prepared to run because he's going to be pissed."

Several of the women say, "Yeah." One says, "He deserved it."

"But let's say you're at a family party, and Uncle Bob has had one too many. He grabs your arm and starts blathering about how beautiful you are, and he doesn't let go. This is the time to just break his grip. No need to make him see stars."

One woman says, "How do you know my uncle?" And everyone laughs, although I don't think it's funny. There are too many Uncle Bobs in the world. I'd still give him a little pop to the chin, uncle or not.

"Not every situation warrants the same degree of violence from you. That is why we show you multiple ways to remove yourself from a situation and scale your actions accordingly. Let's take a water break and then meet back on the mat in five to review last week's lesson."

During the break, a couple of women come over to say hi, pet Rae and tell me how wonderful the class, Annette, and Luca are. I introduce myself by showing them the message on my tablet.

Before they can ask me a bunch of questions, it's time to return to the mat.

"Last Tuesday, we learned how to defend against the choke hold," Luca says, as I feel the blood drain from my face.

Inhaling deeply, I try to control the panic I feel rising in my chest. This is why you are here. Pay attention. Rae, who is lying on my feet lifts her head, tilting her face towards me. She can feel my anxiety. I take another deep breath and rub her throat, trying to reassure her that I'm okay, even though I am not.

"We covered a frontal and rear assault plus a chokehold with you pressed against a wall. Annette and I will demonstrate each defensive maneuver again, first talking through the move as we perform it slowly and then at full speed in a typical situation. After that, we'll break into pairs and practice. So first the frontal assault."

I watch as Luca steps in front of Annette and wraps his arms around her neck. He talks about her tucking her chin to her chest, then diving her head and shoulders down between his arms and coming up on the outside of his outstretched arms. He calls it making a "J." Dive down, then sweep up and out. A "J." The move is finished with an open palm slap to the ear. I'm concentrating on her every move, my heart racing and my breath coming in rapid gasps. This is the exact situation I faced with Charlie when he lost his mind.

"Now, in real-time."

Luca takes several steps back from Annette, who is trying

to look calm. Then Luca rushes at her.

"Crazy bitch," he yells. "I'm going to kill you."

I watch in horror, a high-pitched ringing in my ears, as his arms reach out for her throat. He wraps his hands around her throat as he keeps screaming obscenities at her. He starts shaking her as he yells, then blackness engulfs me, and I am gone.

She slumps forward at the waist and then falls over me, landing on the floor with a thud. I'm pinned under her body but can wriggle free. Woof. Woof. Woof. My girl. My girl. The man comes rushing over. He kneels beside her. He turns his face and places his cheek by Lizzy's nose.

"She's breathing. Someone call 911."

I crawl between the man and Lizzy. I smell her face. I lick her cheek. I lay down next to my girl.

"Your mommy is going to be okay. She just fainted."

"Who are you talking to?" a woman asks.

"The dog."

The woman shakes her head. The man rubs my head before standing. I like him. He smells like Champ. Champ howls by the door at the sound of the siren. I pop up and tilt my head. The sound is growing louder, coming closer. I want to howl, too, but I don't. Instead, I lick my girl's face. I lick and lick, and I'm rewarded with her hand coming up and pushing my face away. She opens her eyes. I am so happy. My tail thumps on the floor. She lifts her head and buries her face next to my good ear.

"Good girl," she whispers over and over again, in a voice only I can hear.

Four men who smell like smoke, walk through the group of women. The oldest of the men comes over and kneels next to me.

"Who do we have here? Does anyone know the dog's name?"

I look around at all the women. They are shaking their heads.

"The woman is new here. Her name is Lizzy. She doesn't speak. That's normal for her. Other than that, I don't know anything about her. She didn't tell me her dog's name."

Lizzy. Dog. They are talking about us. The man who smells like smoke rubs my back. Then I smell something else. A treat!

"Come on. We're going to wait over here while my friends check out your mommy."

I'm not sure what he is saying but he takes my leash and pulls me away. Once we are over by the shoes, which I enjoy smelling, he gives me the treat. It's hard and dry. It smells like it's been in his smoky pocket for a very long time. I finish it quickly, then try to return to Lizzy, but the smoky man is holding me. He is saying things in a calm voice. I do not feel calm. I want to be with my girl. I cry and whine, but no one cares.

Chapter Six

Five Years Ago – July

Honeymoon sex had done the trick. Six weeks after our return, morning sickness reared its ugly head. I would puke up my breakfast on the way to work, pulling over, opening the door, and letting it fly. Then depending on what was being cooked in the hospital kitchen (the smell of fish was particularly nauseating), I'd puke again. By lunchtime, I was starving. I'd devour my nutritious lunch only to have it come back up hours later. I had to move my office out of the kitchen and down the hall where the smell of food had less of an impact, and my retching didn't disturb the staff. Down eight pounds, I felt exhausted all the time. Around three every day, I had to fight the urge to put my head on my desk and take a nap.

My mother-in-law wanted me to quit my job, reminding me often that I didn't need to work. I should focus on one thing and one thing only … caring for my body during this "difficult time." I must admit that after repeated trips to the hospital bathroom, I did want to resign, drive home, and go to bed for the next six months but I'd be damned if I'd let Catherine win *this* battle.

We were living in Charlie's two-bedroom condo in Dana Point overlooking the harbor. The distant sound of the waves crashing against the breakwater and the constant ocean breeze did wonders for my body, but mostly my soul. Our compact balcony had two white wicker chairs and a matching table that held a collection of succulents in colorful pots. As soon as I walked in the door, I'd pry my swollen feet out of my sensible shoes, pour myself a tall glass of lemon/lime bubbly, grab a stack of Saltine Crackers and move to the balcony. I'd prop my feet up on the other chair and stare out over the boat-filled harbor to the ocean beyond.

Charlie usually arrived an hour or two later, depending on the surfing conditions. Before he would head home, he'd call, asking if I was craving something … pickles and ice cream, banana pancakes. Ice cream always came back up and pickles were not my favorite, but for some reason, I couldn't eat enough broccoli, which was a disappointment to Charlie since *he* craved pickles and ice cream. Today was no different. While I was watching a sailboat leave its dock, my phone pinged.

"Hey, Babe. Any must haves? The waves suck and I'm heading home."

I thought for a moment before replying. "How about watermelon?" Watermelon slice emoji.

"Sure. At least if you throw it up it will be colorful." Then a series of emojis … green puking happy face, tongue out silly happy face. Monkey with hands over eyes.

I sent back a thumbs up and a smiley face with a tongue sticking out. Emojis were our love language.

He sent back a smiley face with heart-shaped eyes, and the conversation was over.

An hour later I was enjoying cold watermelon and true to form, an hour after that, I was throwing it all up. But Charlie had been right, the color was awesome.

From the moment we found out I was pregnant Charlie couldn't do enough for me. A pillow for my feet. A back rub. Water, morning or night. Whenever I'd wake up to pee, Charlie would wake up enough to ask, "Are you okay?"

I told him that peeing all the time was normal and he didn't have to wake up when I did. But he said he wanted to start training early for the big moment. He had read, "What to Expect When You're Expecting" and wanted to pack the hospital bag immediately. No such thing as being too prepared, he'd said. I was more relaxed, especially since I worked at a hospital eight hours a day. Catherine was not relaxed. She treated me like a porcelain figurine, fragile and liable to break at any minute, barking out commands to Charlie to assist me like I was an invalid.

After our honeymoon, we were invited for Sunday dinner at Charlie's parents' estate. Somehow this one invitation morphed into an obligation and the next thing I knew, we were spending every Sunday afternoon with Catherine and Robert. Since Charlie surfed first thing in the morning, it didn't disrupt what was important to him. Robert and Charlie would withdraw to the media room where they would watch the game of the week—baseball, golf, basketball—while Mac made sure their glasses were never empty.

I was not thrilled for several reasons … more time with Catherine telling me what to do, what not to eat, and watching my every move. Weekends were supposed to be our time, I had told Charlie, to no avail. We have all day Saturday, minus morning surfing, he'd said, and that had been the end of that.

My friends at work would listen to me complain and then tsk tsk. Poor little rich girl. Her mother-in-law showers her with gifts of new maternity clothes every month, brings manicurists to the house for a mani/pedi before dinner, and has the cook prepare special bland dishes that are supposed to "stay down" and mostly they do. Yes, poor, poor me. While I did appreciate her gifts, especially the pedicures—after all, my mother only sent cards— there was something off about all her attention.

I felt like I was simply the vessel that would bring her precious grandchild safely to shore. I had the distinct feeling that if Catherine could have carried and given birth to her own grandchild, as weird as that would have been, she would have jumped at the opportunity, casting me aside.

By mid-July, my morning sickness had subsided enough

that I could eat again. I craved salty things like chips and peanuts, the saltier the better. I was halfway through a short stack of Pringles when my phone pinged.

"Can you meet me at Las Brisas?" Margarita, chips, salsa, bug-eyed emojis.

"Sure. What time?" Clock emoji.

"I'm already here, so as soon as you can. The waves were lame. Now that you can eat again, let's have an early dinner."

Thumbs up emoji.

"Wear a nice dress. I have a surprise for you after dinner." Happy face emoji.

"Intrigued." Happy face with heart-shaped eyes emoji.

Forty-five minutes later, dressed in my most recent gift from Catherine, a summery floral-print dress that flowed around my protruding belly, I walked into Las Brisas, our favorite oceanfront restaurant in Laguna Beach, and found Charlie on the back patio near the firepit. What remained of the chips and salsa were on the table, and he was halfway through a slushy margarita. He stood when I came in and gave me an excited hug, tipping me from side to side.

"You're in a good mood."

He nodded and motioned that I should sit. The waiter came and I ordered an iced tea, before picking at the last of the chips. Charlie was all antsy in his seat, waiting for the server to leave.

"I'm jumping out of my skin with excitement."

I laughed. "I can see that. Did you win the lottery or something?"

"Better," he said, his smile brighter than the blazing sun that was still hours away from setting.

I couldn't imagine what he was talking about. "Tell me."

"I'd rather show you," he said, downing the rest of his margarita.

"So, show me, then." I had been infected with his excitement.

"It's not here. We need to drive," he said, sounding disappointed.

"Then let's go." I didn't think I could stand the suspense.

"Really? Don't you need to eat something?"

I shook my head as I pulled out a plastic bag of Pringles from my bag.

Charlie jumped up. "Alright." He threw a wad of cash on the table and then helped me up. "Let's take my car. We'll grab yours up on the way home. Maybe we'll have dinner here then."

We walked past the waiter on the way out, who had my tea. While the valet was fetching Charlie's car, the waiter transferred my drink into a to-go cup.

I happily sipped my drink as we drove north on Pacific Coast Highway. After only about a mile, Charlie handed me a scarf.

"Tie this over your eyes."

"You want me blindfolded?" I shook my head.

NO WORDS BETWEEN US

"Babe, be a good sport," he prodded. "It's going to be great."

I sighed before putting the scarf over my eyes and tying the ends together at the back of my head. "Happy?"

"Very. We're almost there."

I felt the car slow, and we made a left turn. Based on my knowledge of the area, I knew we couldn't go very far before we'd hit the edge of a cliff or a beach. Maybe he had something romantic planned at his favorite surf spot. I tilted my head back to peer under the scarf.

"Hey. No cheating," Charlie said, taking another left, then a right before stopping.

I started to take the scarf off, but Charlie grabbed my hand. "Not yet."

"Really?"

Staring at the backside of the scarf, I waited, wondering what this was all about. Charlie opened my door, then taking my hand, pulled me out of the car. The air was heavily scented with salt and seaweed and the boom of the crashing waves made me think we were on a cliff overlooking the ocean.

"Now?"

"Nope."

He led me up a concrete path that I could see by looking down. We stopped and keys jangled. Walking through a door, this mystery place greeted us with silence except for the muted sound of waves crashing. Holding my arm, Charlie walked me straight ahead. Looking under the scarf at my feet, I learn the place has plank flooring the color of driftwood. By turning my head, I catch glimpses of white walls but nothing else. Finally, we came to a halt.

"Almost there." Charlie's excitement pulsed like the bass beat of a techno jam.

This really must be something.

The sound of a sliding door opening preceded a blast of ocean air and the return of the percussion of the waves.

"Okay, now!" Charlie shouted over the din.

I pulled the scarf away and was assaulted by blinding white light. Once my eyes adjusted, the scene morphed into a cloudless sapphire sky and sparkling blue/green water. Charlie was standing on an expansive deck, surrounded by waist-high glass panels, one arm up in the air and one arm down like he was a model on a game show, presenting the next prize. I must have had a bewildered look on my face because Charlie's arms dropped, and he rushed back inside.

"Well? What do you think?"

Looking around, I found myself standing in an amazing great room. A modern kitchen with a huge island made of white marble melded into what I imagined would be the family room complete with a white stone fireplace. The entire wall between the house and the outdoor deck was floor-to-ceiling glass, which I later learned folded like an accordion to bring the outside in.

"Did you rent this place for the weekend or something?" I knew that was doubtful since there was no furniture.

"No. Guess again," he teased.

"Is this a friend's house? Another of your parents' houses?" They did have four houses that I knew of, so I wouldn't have been surprised.

"Nope." Charlie was enjoying himself.

"Then what? Why are we here?"

"This," he said, arms outstretched, spinning slowly in a circle, "is our new home."

I took a step backward. "What?"

"It's ours. All of it," Charlie stood like a proud peacock.

The enormity of this new reality took a minute to sink in. He couldn't be serious.

"You bought a house without me?" I was flabbergasted. Just last night we were looking at real estate ads.

"Surprise! Isn't it awesome?"

"Charlie. We can't afford this." I remembered how much the small cottages were in Laguna Canyon miles from the water. We couldn't even afford those houses. How was this even possible?

Charlie waved away my comment as if it were an annoying gnat. "It's fine. It's all been taken care of."

I knew Charlie had money, but this was probably a six-million-dollar home, maybe more.

"Jesus, Charlie."

It took a moment for Charlie to pick up on the fact that I was not pleased.

"Really? You don't love it. Look, the ocean is right there. I can check out the waves without leaving the house. And at low tide, there is a beach where the kids can play. It's four bedrooms, and four bathrooms, with a two-car garage with lots of room for bikes, surfboards, and kid stuff. How can you not like it?"

"I didn't say I didn't like it. It's amazing, really it is. What I said was, we can't afford it."

The place was beautiful but so modern. Everything was white with shades of gray. I had pictured my first house to be a cozy bungalow with a covered porch overlooking a small, fenced lawn where the children and dogs would play. I would sit on the porch in my wicker chair, sipping a glass of wine in the late afternoon sun, talking to any neighbors who chanced to walk by. Here my front yard was the entirety of the Pacific Ocean, a small patch of sand at low tide thirty feet below, in a neighborhood of people who'd never be walking past my deck.

I watched as Charlie's balloon of joy slowly deflated. My unenthusiastic response had laid waste to his big surprise. I desperately wanted to sit down, but there was no furniture, so I lowered myself slowly to the floor, leaned against one of the bright white walls, and stared into the glare.

Charlie dropped down next to me and took my hand.

"Babe, look at that view," he said softly. "Imagine making coffee each morning, sitting on a white leather couch right here with blue pillows the color of the ocean. In the summer, we can open up the entire wall. It will be like living on a ship," he said, pointing at the wall-to-wall, floor-to-ceiling expanse of glass.

I groaned. The image of living on a ship brought back memories of morning sickness.

"In the winter we'll have a fire. We can sit here with our feet up on a table made of driftwood and glass as the waves crash on the rocks below."

"You've picked out all the furniture, too?" I asked grumpily.

"No, no. I'm just trying to paint a picture."

Shaking my head I asked, "How can we possibly afford this?"

"That's the best part. It's not going to cost us a penny. Not one dime."

And that's when it hit me. Charlie hadn't picked out this house. Catherine had. Suddenly I needed fresh air. "Help me up," I said hoarsely, stretching out my arms for an assist.

Charlie leaped up like he was popping up on his surfboard. "What's the matter? Are you going to be sick? I thought you were over morning sickness."

Once standing, I rushed outside. Pressing my swollen belly to the glass panel, I clasped the patinaed copper railing. I gagged and heaved, but nothing came up. I was hyperventilating and having difficulty catching my breath. Charlie rubbed my back, standing helpless and impotent, whispering "There, there."

After a full minute, the sea air blasting my face took away the feeling of nausea and I concentrated on breathing slowly until I regained control of my emotions.

"Your parents bought this." It was a statement, not a question.

Charlie nodded and smiled. "Of course. We could never afford this place. We just have to maintain it and pay the property taxes, which are nothing to laugh at, but we can afford *that*."

"And let me guess, your mom picked this place."

Charlie shrugged.

"It's an amazing house. Right on the water. She knew I wanted to be close to the beach. Now I can go down the stairs and be riding the waves in minutes. I'll be home more since there's a break right here," he said pointing up the coast.

Great. Your mom has made all your dreams come true. But what about what I want?

"I thought we were going house hunting together. I was looking forward to that. Why would you let her do this?"

"Why wouldn't I? We are going to live at the beach. It has four bedrooms for our growing family," he said, reaching out to touch my belly.

"This doesn't feel right," I said, turning away from him and looking back out at the water.

"This is what rich people do. They help their children. Mom and Dad will probably want to pay for our children's education as well. Are you going to have a problem with that?" he asked, his tone taking on a belligerence I hadn't heard before.

"I don't know." I had toyed with the idea of homeschooling but now pictured an elite prep school where children wore smart little uniforms, and first graders were groomed to be tomorrow's CEOs. The mental picture made me shudder.

Charlie gently turned me back towards him. "Look. This can be strange ... all this money and generosity, but it's what they do, so I say, let them. Why fight it? We get to live here."

"Here" was spectacular. My co-workers' words, "Poor little rich girl" bounced around in my head. Who in their right mind would complain about being given a beach house? And yet, I was sad. First Catherine co-opted my wedding and now she's micro-managing my pregnancy and deciding where we're going to live. At least I'll be able to decorate, maybe paint some of these walls, and make this house a home. I had to admit, a white couch with blue pillows would be perfect.

"Charlie. I'm sorry I didn't react more positively. Shock, raging hormones ... I don't know. I guess this place is ... alright," I smiled. "I'll try to get used to this view."

Charlie pulled me in for a hug, wrapping his arms around me. He whispered in my ear, "I knew you'd love it, because it's totally awesome, right?"

"Yes. Totally awesome," I whispered as I pulled out of his embrace. "Let's go for a walk on the beach ... our beach?"

"Absolutely. I'll grab a couple of beach towels from the car—" Charlie's phone rang cutting him off. When he answered, all he said was, "Okay" before heading to the front door. I had a direct line of sight as the door swung open and there she was, Catherine. Just as I was wrapping my head around the idea that this was our new home, here comes Catherine to mark her territory like the alpha wolf she is. Nausea swirled and I turned to lean over the railing. The next thing I knew, Catherine was at my side, asking if I was okay. Did I need some water? Yelling at Charlie to help me sit down. When I started to let myself drop to the ground, Catherine screamed Charlie's name and the two of them kept me upright.

"The stairs," Catherine vocalized like a major general.

Seated on the stairs, elbows on my knees, head in my hands, I could hear them whispering.

"Should we take her to the doctor? She looks pale," Catherine worried.

"She's fine. It's just the excitement over the house. She can't believe it," Charlie lied.

At least he got that last part right.

"Have you taken her upstairs yet? Maybe that will make her feel better."

"Not yet. We've spent the entire time staring at the view. It's breathtaking. How did you find this place?"

Catherine laughed softly. "Mother has her ways."

Yes, she does, I thought. "What's upstairs? Any furniture?" I asked hopefully, as all I wanted to do was curl up in a ball and fall asleep. Maybe Catherine would be gone when I woke up.

"Sounds like she's feeling better. I can't wait to show you the nursery. It's just perfect," Catherine oozed.

Alarms went off inside my head. No. She didn't. I awkwardly stood up, pushing away any help from Charlie or his mother. No one could move past me, so I was the first one at the top of the stairs. There was a wide hallway that ran the length of the house, parallel to the beach below. All the rooms were on the beach side of the hall, with their doors open and light streaming in through the windows that overlooked the glistening ocean. A quick look inside the first two rooms revealed nothing. No furniture, white walls, and white carpet all made brilliant by the white light. The third room, the primary bedroom, was as large as the living room and kitchen in my first apartment. Normally I would have explored the room, checked out the closet and the attached bathroom. But my heart was racing as I neared the last door. I hoped against hope that I was wrong. That it was just another empty room, a blank palette that I could liven up with colorful furniture, pillows, wall coverings, anything to give these lifeless rooms some character and warmth.

But I wasn't wrong. I stood in the doorway and held the doorjambs, one in each hand, like I was going down with the Titanic.

The nursery. It was completely furnished. Seafoam green sheer curtains with seahorses cut the bright light enough that I could take it all in. A white crib with matching changing table/dresser drawers. A rocking chair and lamp sat in the corner facing the windows. Cute prints of cartoon sea creatures were framed in white-washed wood. A low bookshelf was already filled with books and toys. A pile of darker green pillows, also with sea creatures, were piled in the corner. What was there left for me to do but squat and drop the baby on the white carpet. I wanted to scream, but all I could do was hold onto the doorjambs as if my life depended on it.

Charlie caught up with me, pulling my arm down so he could push past me. "Oh wow. Did you do all this, mom?"

"Do you like it?" Catherine asked with obvious satisfaction standing next to me. "I thought green was the best color since we don't know whether it's a boy or a girl. And all the sea creatures were a natural addition since you're at the beach. You won't even need one of those sound machines. You can just open the window and he'll be lulled to sleep by the sound of real crashing waves."

Charlie bent down and looked at the books and toys. "Hey. These are my old books."

Catherine was in her element. "I kept them all these years. And look. Your Hot Wheels collection. They are probably worth a fortune, but nothing's too good for my grandson."

Charlie looked up at me. He was backlit and glowed like an angel. "Babe, go sit in the rocking chair so I can take your picture."

I don't know how I made it from the door to the rocking chair on rubber legs. I smiled for the picture, but my mind was elsewhere. The wedding, the house, and now the nursery. What was Catherine going to take next … Charlie? The baby?

The plot of an old movie I'd watched with Mom, Rosemary's Baby, crept into my head, where the pregnant mother is manipulated into giving birth to the devil's child. Charlie wasn't the devil, and Catherine wasn't part of a Satanic cult, but I certainly felt manipulated like poor Rosemary.

While Catherine and my husband buzzed like bees over Charlie's childhood books as if they were fragrant flowers, I was able to calm myself with slow, deep breaths, willing my anger to subside as I rocked back and forth. The room *was* Pinterest-perfect as if Martha Stewart had designed it herself … maybe she had. Finally, I thought I was ready to say something without revealing how hurt I felt.

"The nursery is beautiful, Catherine," I said, trying to sound positive and grateful.

"Do you love it?" she asked, looking at the crib, not at me.

"What's not to love?" I admitted, except for the fact that it should have been me who decorated the room for our baby, not my mother-in-law. "It's too much. You really shouldn't have." And I meant it. It really *was* too much, and she really *shouldn't* have, but what could I do now? Make her take it all back?

Catherine brushed my comments away as if they were nothing more than gossamer wisps of smoke. "It was nothing."

Maybe it was nothing to you, I thought. But it meant something to me.

Chapter Seven

Pat, Pat – Jump Up

Wet. My face is wet. Rae is licking me. I move my hand up to push her away and that's when I realize I'm on the ground with Rae. No wonder she is licking my face. Why am I on the ground? Where am I? I open my eyes and I'm looking up at an industrial-looking ceiling for a brief second before Rae obstructs my view by sniffing my face. I put my arms around her, lifting my head slightly so that I can whisper in her ear, "Good girl." Then Rae is pulled away and her face is replaced by a paramedic.

"Hi Ma'am. My name is Brian and I'm with Pine City Fire. I understand that you can't speak. Is that correct?"

I nod. Then Luca taps Brian on the shoulder and passes him my tablet.

"Is this how you normally communicate?"

I nod again.

"Great," he says and hands me my tablet. "I need to ask you a few questions. What is your name?"

I type, "Lizzy Mueller."

"Do you know where you are, Lizzy?"

I nod and type, "Jiu-Jitsu class."

Brian looks around and smiles. "Yes. And what day is it?"

I have to think. It's a Wednesday, but I'm not sure of the date. Normally I would look at my phone. "It's a Wednesday in mid-June. Not sure of the exact date."

Brian nods. "If I am not working, I don't know the date, either. Now I'm going to check your vitals and make sure you're okay. Do you have pain anywhere?"

Mostly I'm embarrassed and want to sit up. I have to think for a second. Take a mental inventory. That's when I become aware of the throbbing in my head. I touch my head lightly and feel a bump. I point to the place on my head just inside my hairline above my right eye. Brian gently touches my head until he comes to the spot that makes me flinch.

"She has a quarter-size bump on her skull above her right eye. The skin isn't broken," he says, as the second paramedic records his observations.

Next, he takes out a small pen light and checks my pupils. "Pupils are equal and reacting normally. That's good." He gives me a reassuring smile. "Any numbness or tingling in your arms or legs?"

I shake my head and am rewarded with a thumbs up.

"Would you like to sit up?"

I nod, and then he pulls me to a sitting position making it easier for the other paramedic, Jackson, according to the name on his jacket, to secure a blood pressure cuff and slide a pulse/oxygen meter over my index finger. Moments later, Jackson calls out the readings, then gives me a thumbs up as well. While all this is going on, I look around for Rae and find her with another firefighter, straining at her collar to be with me. Poor Rae. She must be freaking out. I pick up my tablet and write, "Can you bring me my dog?" Then show it to Brian.

"Soon. According to witnesses, you appear to have fainted. Do you know why?"

Yes, I think. Watching Luca charge Annette, the same way Charlie had charged me, took me back to that awful day. My body must have freaked out. But I don't want to explain this to these guys, so I shake my head. I know what happened. I don't need to tell them. It's not a medical condition. It was a massive panic attack.

"You have a bump on your head from falling off the bench. Does this sound right?"

I nod.

"We'd like to transport you to the hospital to be evaluated. Maybe they can find out why you fainted."

I shake my head no.

"Can you sign this AMA form?" Brian turns to Jackson,

who hands him a clipboard.

Head cocked in confusion, I mouth the word, "What?"

"Sorry. We use a lot of acronyms in the fire department. It's an Against Medical Advice form. It simply states that we recommended a hospital visit and you declined."

He hands me the clipboard, and I sign my name. Then I point to Rae.

"Sure. Hey Carson. Release the dog."

Carson unclips Rae from her leash, and she makes a mad dash right to me, jumping into my lap and licking my throat as I tip up my head. Her butt and tail are a blur of motion as she expresses her happiness. I bury my face in her fur and rub her backside until she calms down.

"She's happy you're okay," says Luca, who has walked over and knelt beside me. "I'm happy, too. People do on occasion get injured here, but it's usually out on the mat, not sitting on the bench."

I'm so embarrassed. I just want to go home. Coming here was a bad idea. Pushing Rae off my lap, I slowly stand. My head is a bit woozy, but I'm still determined to go home.

"Why don't you sit in my office? I have a couch in there. I don't think you should drive home yet. Maybe wait a bit until we know you are fine."

I shake my head, but paramedic Brian agrees.

"That's a good idea. Walk around. Make sure you feel okay."

Picking up my tablet, I write. "I feel fine. Just my head is sore."

"Humor me," Luca insists. "At least wait ten minutes or so before you drive home. Just to be sure."

Reluctantly, I nod. I grab my daypack and with Rae "herding" me along by pushing her nose into my calf, I head to the open door that faces out into the gym. A huge picture window connects the inside of the office to the rest of the room so that even if the door is closed, anyone standing on the mat could see inside. This makes me feel better. The last thing I want to do is be in some guy's office, alone, with the door closed.

There is an ugly brown couch against the wall by the door and I lower myself slowly into the corner, my head beginning to throb. Dog hair on the cushions is my hint that this is a dog-friendly couch. I pat, pat, the cushion and Rae leaps onto the couch, curling up next to me, her head on my lap. A moment later, Champ walks in. He assesses the situation and saunters over. He gives Rae a quick sniff and then joins us on the couch next to Rae. This must be his couch. Rae lifts her head and looks over her shoulder at him before deciding to ignore his presence.

I'm busy with my girl. I can't pay attention to this other dog. As long as he stays where he is, we'll be fine. My girl is calm now. Her breathing is normal. Her heart beats softly. I was scared for her, but everything is okay now. The man comes in and my girl's heart rate quickens. She starts to stand but my head is on her lap. The man walks over with a glass of water and something in his closed hand. Smells like those white pills that my girl carries in her bag.

"I thought you might need a couple of aspirin." Luca holds out the glass of water and opens his palm.

I make the sign for thank you, and he replies, "You're welcome."

After downing the aspirin, I mouth, and sign, "Do you know sign language?"

Luca smiles. "Just a few basics. I had a deaf student once. She taught me a few signs. She was also very good at reading lips."

I give him a thumbs up.

Luca grabs the top of his desk chair and rolls it around until he's in front of me. He takes a seat. "I want to talk to you about what happened today. While it's the first time someone has fainted, it's not the first time a woman has had a visceral reaction to our situational learning. It's usually because of a traumatic experience from the past, which is why they come to the class in the first place. Am I close?"

At first, I'm taken aback. I want to pull away, deny the truth, and then run out of here as fast as I can. But what he said is true. So true. And it's the reason I'm here. If I freeze up or pass out the next time Charlie loses his cool and comes at me—and there will be a next time—I could end up dead, literally, dead, not just speechless. Finally, I nod.

"We should talk about it. First off, you should know that

you were watching class number thirteen out of fifteen. If you had started with the first class, you wouldn't have had to watch me charge Annette. We don't do that until the last few classes. Does that make sense?"

I nod. But I still don't know how I will react when someone … anyone, puts their hands around my throat. I pick up my tablet and begin typing.

"I came to this class to learn self-defense. My husband strangled me. Between what he did and the intubation tube damage, I can no longer speak. I've been hiding here in Pine City for the past three years. I don't know how he will find me, but I'm sure he will. I don't have time for a thirteen-week class. He could show up tomorrow. I need to be ready. Is there anything you can do to help me?"

The entire time I'm typing, Luca sits patiently. I finally hand him the tablet and now it's my turn to wait. Luca nods as he reads and then looks up.

"I'm sorry for what you've been through. Strangulation is one of the deadliest forms of domestic violence. Many of the women who take our classes have had similar experiences. Let me talk with Annette. Maybe we can give you some private lessons over the next couple of weeks until the new class starts. We'll concentrate on breaking choke holds, but we will work into it slowly. Would that be something you'd be interested in trying?"

I nod.

"I'm thinking we could meet you immediately after this

class. That way Annette and I would already be here. Would that work for you?"

I nod again.

"Okay. Let me talk to Annette. I think she's still here."

Luca leaves and Champ follows. I'm feeling better. I don't know if it's the aspirin or Luca's calm demeanor that has relaxed me. I stand and walk over to a narrow console table against the wall behind Luca's desk where there are several framed photos. I pick up the first one. It's a family portrait. The mother is small and Japanese, wearing a white gi with a black belt tied around her waist. The father is much taller, a black man, also wearing a white gi with a black belt. Standing in front of his parents is a young Luca—maybe ten years old—the perfect blend of his Japanese mother and his black father. He, too, is wearing a white gi, although his belt is green. I replace the photo and look at the next one. Luca is a teenager in this photo, wearing a brown belt and engaged in what looks like a tournament. The rest of the photos are of Luca as an adult, none include pictures of Luca with a woman. Hmmm. Stop it. I tell myself. Just stop.

I hear talking and turn around. Annette and Luca walk into the office.

"Good news. Annette is available," Luca says.

I nod and mouth, "Great." Then I walk back to the couch and pick up my tablet. I type, "When can we start, and how much?" I show what I've written to Luca, then to Annette.

Luca looks at Annette. "Luca explained the situation. I

understand what you are going through. My husband did a number on me. He broke my arm and almost killed me. He's in prison now, but he'll be out someday, and I vowed I'd be ready if he ever came back. So, let's do this. There are different classes here almost every day. I attend three evening classes a week, Monday, Wednesday, and Friday. Luca and I will stay after those classes and show you a few moves. Then, when the next round of Women Empowered starts, you'll sign up for the series. How does that sound?"

I mouth the word, "Great" and then I make the unofficial sign for money ... holding up my hand and rubbing my thumb against my fingertips. I mouth the words, "How much?" in case they don't understand, but Luca does.

"Annette and I talked about that, too. As long as you sign up for the series and pay for that, then we are happy to stay after our regular classes and give you a head start on some basic moves for free."

"Wow. Really?" I mouth.

"As I said, I've been where you are. I'm happy to help out. We'll teach you some moves but then you need to practice them at home. Do you have someone you can practice with? The more you practice, the more the moves will become second nature," says Annette.

I'm thinking of Abby. Maybe even Frank. I nod.

"Great," says Luca. "Our next class is on Friday at six. See you then?"

I nod and sign "Thank You" to both of them.

By the time I'm back home, I'm starving. As soon as we walk in the door, Rae starts talking. Rrrrrrr. She is hungry, too. An hour later, after a glass of wine and salad for me, kibble and hamburger for Rae, we are both snuggled in bed. I'm reading a novel on my tablet while Rae rests her head on my thigh. The glow of my tablet creates a bubble of light around us in the darkness. Rae's paws twitch and move. I'd love to know what she is dreaming about.

My eyes feel scratchy. I'll read to the end of a chapter before turning off the tablet. What a day. My mind wanders away from the novel. Replaying the self-defense class, specifically the maneuvers for breaking out of a chokehold, gives me hope. If those women can defend themselves against larger, stronger opponents, then so can I.

Maybe Abby would take the class with me, if not, she might agree to be my practice partner. Frank, too. I can't freeze. I can't panic. I have to be ready.

When the phone rings, I gasp and jump, causing Rae to leap up. I look at the Caller ID. It's Mom. Why is she calling me instead of texting? And why this late? As I press the button to connect the call, a feeling of dread washes over me.

"Sorry to call so late."

She waits as if I'm going to say something.

"Right. Well, it's important. After Charlie came by the house that first time, I thought that would be the end of it since I threatened to call the police. But then he left the flowers with that beautiful note. I'm sorry, but I read the note. It was sweet. I just couldn't throw it away unopened."

Just like all of those letters he sent me, care of mom's address, while he was locked up. I'd wanted her to throw them away unread. But she didn't.

"Anyway, he's been around several times. Don't worry. He hasn't come to the door or talked to me again, but he's been hanging around the neighborhood as if he hopes you'll come driving by. He's not doing anything wrong, just walking up and down the street. He doesn't stop or even linger in front of the house. He just walks by two or three times a day. And at night, I get this creepy feeling he's watching the house. I haven't said anything to him but I'm thinking of calling the police. I don't know if there is anything they can do since he's not breaking the law. I just thought you should know. How are you holding up?"

I text her. "I'm taking a self-defense class."

There is a long pause. I can imagine the text message popping up on her screen.

"Oh. That's a good idea."

I text, "Thanks for letting me know about Charlie. You should call the police. If he keeps showing up, you'll need a restraining order or something."

"Yes. Yes. I should do that. He gives me the willies. When he was talking through the door that first time, he said he was all better, but I don't believe it. His mother probably bought off those fancy doctors. You know … he's obsessed with you. I told him to move on. The last thing he said was, 'I'll find her. I'll make her understand.'"

Hearing those words sent a chill down my spine. I better be ready.

Her heart is beating faster. I put a paw on her thigh and whine. She rubs my head, but her heart is still racing. Finally, she turns off the voice thing and the room is quiet. She rearranges the pillows and lies down. I move around her feet and curl up against her stomach. She drapes her arm over my body and pulls me in close. She whispers into my good ear, 'I love you.' I don't know what those words mean, but she says them all the time. It calms her, so I like those words. I wish I could say them back to her.

Chapter Eight

Five Years Ago – August

We'd been in the new house now for a little over a month, and I'd come to love it, especially after I put my personal stamp on the place. Catherine wasn't the only one who can mark territory like a dog. Mine, mine, mine.

To Charlie, the ocean was all he needed, so I was able to pick all the furniture … from our new king-size bed to the white faux leather couch with deep blue throw pillows. Charlie had that right. I bought colorful photographs of marine life and hung them on the walls to break up the vast expanses of white.

I admit I went a little crazy at a local nursery. We now have a braided Benjamina Ficus tree in a deep blue pot in the corner of the great room, and an Aloe Vera plant in the kitchen—it's good for burns. An assortment of adorable succulents in colorful pots gathered in little groupings throughout the house added their splashes of color. Catherine questioned whether all this "wildlife" would be good for the baby. I tuned her out, something I was becoming quite proficient at, although I wish Charlie could do the same. I've even gotten over the fact that Catherine decorated the nursery, although I did move things around and added a few girl toys. She didn't notice.

The summer heat tortured my heavy breasts and expanding stomach creating pools of sweat in new, uncomfortable places. While the hospital where I worked was air-conditioned, and my car was air-conditioned, the walk between the two had me sweating like a sumo wrestler in a steam bath.

As soon as I came home, I'd open the sliding wall and step out onto the balcony, an "ahhh" escaping my lips as the sea breeze swept back my hair away from my face and dried the sweat on my neck. Once my body temp returned to normal, I'd pour myself a cold glass of mango juice—one of my cravings—and sit outside to open the mail.

Once the sun set or the fog rolled in, the temperature would drop ten more degrees and I'd head back inside. I could count on Charlie walking in the door within an hour after sunset, hair wet and his body smelling of salt and sunscreen. He'd plant a big wet kiss on my cheek before bending over to kiss my belly.

"How are my two favorite people?" he'd ask.

Then I'd give him the full report for the day … what I had for lunch, what strange things I was craving, and whether or not the baby had moved. That last one was very important to Charlie.

He wanted to feel the baby move. To Charlie, the baby was like an alien—foreign and strange—growing inside of me. But once he— the baby is always a "he" to Charlie and Catherine—starts moving and kicking, then Charlie can be part of the experience. It will become real for him.

It was the first week in August and I was thirteen weeks along. There were a few times when I thought I felt something. A fluttering. One time it turned out to be gas, another time, indigestion. According to what I'd read, it was still too early to feel movement. That would come around sixteen weeks, especially for a first-time mom who wasn't sure what baby movement would feel like. Catherine tried to tell me, as did the nurses at the hospital, but knowing what something should feel like is not the same as feeling it. Catherine was almost as bad as Charlie when it came to the whole baby-moving thing. Every Saturday evening she'd send a text. "How's it going? Any kicking yet?" I'd reply, "Not yet." I swear I could hear her groan of disappointment.

My mother, on the other hand, sent cards. Cards, cards, and more cards. Some were appropriate and some were weird … a T-Rex sitting on an egg? What was that about? She always wrote what she thought was an encouraging word or two—what she had done to mitigate the nausea or how she kept cool on The Farm when at 8 months I had made her as "big as a Mac truck"—before returning to her favorite subject, herself. She was nowhere near as excited as Catherine about the prospect of becoming a grandmother. In fact, she told me that 52 was too young to be a grandmother, and I should have waited until she was sixty, which would have made me 41 and in the high-risk category. But again, it was all about her.

The air conditioner was set to a chilly sixty degrees as I drove home from work. Pulling into the garage, I cut the engine and clicked the button to close the garage door behind me. Emerging from my cocoon of coldness into the hot box that was the garage was a shock to my system. I immediately felt uncomfortable. I couldn't wait to escape as I headed to the door that led into the calm, cool, quiet of my home. Halfway there, a stabbing pain low in my belly made me gasp in surprise and had me holding my stomach as I bent over. Beads of sweat popped out on my forehead, as I struggled to make it to the door. Once inside, I forced myself to keep walking until I was standing at the floor-to-ceiling wall of windows. I thought, if I could just get outside where it was cool, I'd be okay. The pain subsided enough for me to stand straighter and open the door. Then another pain had me grasping the edge of the sliding door, my knuckles turning white.

What was happening?

Lowering myself into one of the patio chairs, I concentrated on breathing. This helped, and the cramping became a dull ache more like menstrual cramps. The ocean breeze cooled my brow and the sound of the waves rhythmically crashing on the rocks below helped me calm down. I sat there for at least ten minutes before standing and walking into the house. Retrieving my purse, I returned to the patio deck. Using my phone, I Googled cramping at twelve weeks. The first thing that came up was "round ligament pain," which I'd never heard of before. Upon searching further, I found a better description of what I was feeling … a miscarriage.

No, no, no, no. I tried calling Charlie. I looked at the time. He would still be on his board. Should I call Catherine? Hell no! She was the last person I wanted to call.

My mom was off with her latest and greatest in Canada on another adventure, so I called my doctor. Since it was after hours, I was connected to the answering service. To hell with it, I thought and headed back to the car.

As I was driving myself through the canyon to my hospital, I felt slick wetness like I was having my period. This was bad. This was very bad. After what felt like an eternity, I pulled around to the emergency entrance and parked. Another cramp forced me to clench my teeth as I fought through the pain and continued across the hot parking lot to the sliding glass doors of the emergency entrance.

The emergency reception area was thankfully sparsely populated. As I stepped up to the intake window, another cramp wracked my body, and I felt another gush of blood. When I caught my breath, I was able to speak.

"I'm twelve weeks pregnant and I think I'm having a miscarriage," I managed to say.

As soon as I said the word "miscarriage," the emotions I'd been holding back came gushing forth like the blood, along with a

NO WORDS BETWEEN US

giant sob and a torrent of tears. I never heard the nurse say anything, but she must have because I became aware of gentle hands lowering me into a wheelchair as I continued to cry. Clutching my purse to my chest, I looked down at my lap. I moaned with grief at the sight. My beige pants were stained red between my legs.

No, no, no. This can't be happening. But it was. I needed Charlie. I needed him here with me. As they wheeled me to an available bed, I searched for my phone.

"Can you stand?" the nurse asked, taking my purse and placing it on a side table.

"Yes, I think so."

She steadied me with a hand under my arm as I stood up. She tried to take my phone. I wouldn't let her. I needed to call my husband. She nodded, but I could tell she wasn't happy about it.

I called Charlie but he didn't answer, so I left a message: "Charlie. I'm at the hospital. My hospital in Laguna Hills. Something is wrong. I think I'm losing the baby. Please come as soon as you can."

Next, I called my friend Sandy who works with me at the hospital. Our shifts overlap for three hours each day. She should still be here at the hospital, I thought as I dialed her number.

I sighed with relief when I heard her voice. "Oh my god, Sandy. I'm in the ER. I'm losing the baby."

"No, Lizzy. No."

Trying not to cry I asked, "Can you come down here?"

"Our ER?"

"Yes. I went home and came back. Charlie is still surfing and hasn't answered his phone. I could use a friendly face."

"Of course. I'll be right there," Sandy said, causing a new rush of tears.

Sandy was holding my hand and crying with me when we heard Charlie's voice yelling at the intake nurse demanding to be let in. I sent Sandy out to smooth things over. When he finally pulled back the curtain and stood at the foot of the bed, he took one look at me before he burst into tears of his own. Sandy appeared in the doorway. I mouthed, "Thank you" before turning to look at my husband.

"Are you okay?" he choked out.

Shaking my head slowly I said softly, "No. We've lost our baby. I'm so sorry."

Charlie climbed onto the bed next to me and pulled me into his arms. He couldn't speak, so he simply rocked me gently as we both cried. Moments later, the doctor came in to explain what was going to happen next.

I was surprised when Charlie asked, "How long do we have to wait until we can try again?"

"Mrs. Bouchard should resume her natural menstrual cycles within four to six weeks—"

Charlie interrupted. "And that means we can start trying again?"

"Technically, yes. But I recommend waiting three to six

months to let her body fully heal and recover. You can talk with your OB/GYN about that at your next appointment."

"That's great. Thank you, doctor." Then turning to me. "Did you hear that? We can try again in three months."

The last thing I wanted to think about was getting pregnant again. All I wanted to do was go home and curl into a little ball and sleep. Maybe I'd wake up and this will have all been a very bad dream.

"Did you call my mother?" Charlie wanted to know.

I shook my head.

"She's going to be devastated. Was it a boy or girl?" Charlie asked, as he swung his legs over the side of the bed and stood.

Oh, my baby is an "it" now that she's gone. I was so angry I couldn't even look at him. I turned away and buried my face in the pillow. When I didn't answer Charlie turned to the doctor.

"We were going to have an ultrasound at our next appointment to find out the sex of the baby. Is there any way to find out now?"

The doctor nodded, then motioned Charlie to step outside the curtained area. I heard their hushed whispers. I didn't want to know the sex of my baby. What difference would it make? My baby was gone. Why was Charlie so desperate to know? My mind went to a dark place. If my baby was a girl, it wouldn't be such a loss, since Catherine had her heart set on a boy.

Charlie pulled the curtain back and sat on the edge of the

bed. Gently, he touched my face and I reluctantly rolled over to face him, dark thoughts swirling like black smoke.

"You're upset. I am, too. I want to know the sex of the baby so we can name him, maybe have a little burial or something. What do you think?"

Suddenly, I felt like a real jerk. I started crying again and managed a sniff and a nod before saying, "That's a lovely idea."

"I need to call Mom. I don't know how I'm going to tell her that you lost the baby. She's going to be heartbroken."

You lost the baby. Before it was, "We're pregnant. We're having a baby." Now instead of "we" it's "you" as in "*You* lost the baby." The pain of his words made me sob. Deep down, Charlie must think the miscarriage was my fault, even though the doctor explained that one in four women have a miscarriage in the first three months. When I asked what could have caused this to happen, the doctor said it was probably a genetic abnormality. The fetus wasn't forming correctly so the body rejected the baby. My body rejected my baby. I moaned.

"Please don't call her yet. I need some time," I said, before patting the side of the bed. "Come back and sit with me."

Charlie looked at me, then at his phone. Slowly he shook his head. "She'll kill me if I don't call. I'll never hear the end of it. She'll want to be here. This was going to be her first grandchild. You have no idea how upset she is going to be."

And there it was … not upsetting his mother was his top priority. From the wedding to the new house, from the mandatory

Sunday dinners to decorating the nursery, Charlie had had a choice—upset his mother or upset me. And each time, he chose his mother over me. Each betrayal felt like a pinprick, drawing a drop of blood, but this time was different. This betrayal, when I needed him the most, was a dagger to my heart.

Chapter Nine

Flat Hand – Stay

We are back at the place with the wonderful smells. There is a wall filled with shoes. My nose is twitching and working hard to take in each unique scent. Lizzy puts her shoes into one of the holes in the wall. I want to stand here and keep sniffing. Someone stepped in horse poop. Someone else walked through the mud. Lizzy pulls me away from the wall. I try sitting down. Lizzy looks back at me and tugs on the leash. Once we are at the bench, she snaps her fingers. I don't want to sit. She snaps again. Okay. I'll sit but first I'll bark. Woof.

"Shhhh," *she says with a finger to her lips.*

Woof. I don't want to sit. She snaps again. I sigh, then sit. She wraps my leash around one of the bench legs. She scratches my head. Then she walks away leaving me alone. I stand up to follow her, but she puts her hand out. I don't want to stay. I want to go play with my girl on the soft, squishy floor. I strain against the leash. The bench moves. Lizzy comes back. She snaps. Then she points down. I sit, then flop onto the cold floor. She rubs my head again. Then shows me her flat hand before returning to the soft floor.

I walked on the soft floor once. A woman they call Annette yelled at me. She said, "No!" and then a bunch of other words I didn't understand, except for the word "dog" which is me. So instead of lying on the soft floor, I lay here by the bench. Here comes Champ. He's free to walk around without a leash. I want to walk around without a leash. I watch him. He doesn't go on the soft floor. Champ's guy comes out of the room. Before he came out, I could see him through the clear wall. He walks over to Champ and gives him a treat. I sit up and bark, woof. I want a treat. He understands. He walks over. He snaps his fingers. I sit. He points down. I lie down. I get the treat. It's a minty, chewy stick. This is going to take some time. I begin to chew.

Rae is now happily occupied, thanks to Luca. I make the sign for "thank you," and he nods. I've had three twenty-minute sessions with Luca and Annette. I can't believe how much I've learned. There are at least three ways to break someone's grip if they are trying to pull me somewhere by my arm. I've learned one way to escape if someone is strangling me from the front, although we've only done this with Annette being the assailant, not Luca. I still need to break a stranglehold from behind, and one where I'm pushed against a wall. But I'm happy with what I've learned so far. In another week, I'll be joining the regular class. Not only has Abby decided to join me, but she's also bringing her daughter. It's never too early to learn how to defend yourself, she explained.

 Luca and I had already started stretching when Annette comes out of the bathroom and walks down the hall toward us. She bows slightly before stepping onto the mat. Today, she is wearing a traditional white gi instead of street clothes since the preceding class was a preparation class for a tournament. The air is still heavy with overtones of sweat and male testosterone.

Yesterday I arrived early and watched the sparring. The place reverberated with grunts and shouts of encouragement as the participants struggled to extricate themselves from various holds. After the class ended, Annette asked if I might be interested in joining the more traditional Jiu-Jitsu class. I shook my head. What I'm learning will be enough; or at least I hope it will be.

Today's class must have been a good workout since Annette's shoulder-length brown hair is slick with sweat. As she walks over to join us, she runs her fingers through her hair before pulling it up into a ponytail. Usually, we shake hands before we start, but when I reach out, she waves me off.

"I'm a disgusting sweat ball," she says, wiping her hands on her white uniform pants.

Having just participated in an hour-long class, Annette is already warmed up.

"Let's go through all the maneuvers for breaking

someone's grip on your arm or wrist. We'll start with a one-handed grip and then a two-handed grip," says Luca.

Annette nods and then steps in front of me. She reaches out with one hand and grabs my arm above my wrist; her palm is up. I turn my arm so that the narrowest part is lined up between her fingertips and thumb. Then in one fluid movement, I bend my elbow as I move my fist toward my chest and my elbow toward her. My arm slides out of her grip between her thumb and fingers.

"Good," says Luca, who is standing next to us. "Now with her palm down."

Annette grabs me again, this time, her palm is on top of my arm, and the opening is facing down. I turn my wrist, and bring my fist toward me, as my elbow slices over her grip. I break free.

"Nice. Do you think you are ready to let me grab your wrist? No yelling, I promise." Luca places a hand over his heart.

I nod. Annette is replaced by Luca in front of me. I stretch out my arm and he grabs my wrist. For an instant, I freeze. His hand is so much larger than Annette's.

As if reading my mind, Luca says, "It doesn't matter who is holding your wrist. The weakness is the same … the gap between the thumb and fingertips."

Turning my arm so the narrowest part of my wrist lines up with the gap, I pull my wrist up to my chest while at the same time pushing my elbow into Luca's chest. I pop free!

I must have had a look of astonishment on my face because Luca says, "See. I told you. Do it again."

He takes hold of my wrist, but this time his hold is tighter. Again, I break free. This is so cool. I mouth the word, "Again."

This time his palm is facing down. I pull my fist toward my stomach, slice my elbow over his grip and I'm free.

"Wow," I mouth and smile.

Luca shakes his head and wags his fingers, before surprising me with a two-handed grab on my right wrist. I take a step forward as my left hand goes over and through Luca's arms to grab my right hand. Pulling up and to my chest, my elbow shoots forward and up, breaking the grip and barely missing his chin.

"Excellent. You've been practicing. That's good. If this had been a real attack, swing that elbow up with more force and you'd have a good chance of catching him hard under the chin. Then run like hell, cuz he's gonna be pissed."

I make a snorting sound that passes for laughter that, based on their wide eyes, shocks both Annette and Luca.

"Was that a laugh?" Annette asks.

I nod.

"Good. You're relaxing," says Annette. "And I might add, even enjoying yourself. I'm going to convince you to join the competitive class yet."

Shaking my head, I shoo away her comment like an annoying gnat.

Luca looks at the clock. "We have time to learn one new move. Let's say you are trying to leave a room. Your back is to this man who is annoying you. You think you're safe because you're leaving. Then he comes up behind you, wraps his arms around your waist, and starts pulling you back."

I can imagine this happening, so I nod.

"Remember, you don't use force against force. You take and use his energy against him. If he's bending you forward, you'll throw him forward. If he's dragging you backward, then you'll use that momentum and drop him behind you. In this situation, he has come up behind you and is pulling you away. Your arms are free." He waves Annette over.

Annette stands in front of Luca, facing away from him. Luca wraps his arms around Annette's waist.

"The first step is to bend over at the waist. Your legs may or may not be touching the ground. The important thing is to spread your legs apart. Then reach between your legs and grab one of your assailant's legs."

Charlie's legs.

I watch as Annette bends. She appears slack, like a rag doll. Then she spreads her legs apart and reaches through to grab one of Luca's legs with both hands.

"Because I'm already moving backward, this next part uses my momentum to send me down. Annette is going to lean back into me and at the same time, pull my leg up through her legs. If she does this hard and fast, she can break my leg. But you are going to be nice, right?"

Annette turns her head and looks up at Luca with a sugary sweet smile. "Of course, dear."

Suddenly, Luca fell on his back with Annette on top of him. Annette springs up and moves away.

"Was that nice enough for you?" she says with a snarky grin.

I point at my chest. "My turn," I mouth.

After going through the motions one step at a time, I'm finally ready. First, Annette grabs me. I bend, spread my legs, grab, lean, and pull. Then, boom, we are both on the ground. I'm so amazed that I don't pop up right away.

"Nice job. Now can you get off of me?"

I roll off and mouth, "Sorry."

"Now it's my turn," says Luca.

Is this going to work on this big guy? Reluctantly, I step in front of Luca and face the wall.

"We'll do this nice and slow. Try not to hurt me," he says as he steps in close and wraps his arms around my waist.

For a second, I don't move. The feeling of his body pressed against mine is not an unpleasant sensation. But then he starts dragging me backward and I snap out of it. Bend, spread, grab, lean, and pull up. Luca goes down on his back like a WWE SmackDown wrestler with a satisfying thud. I land on top of him but this time, I spring up and move away. Rae doesn't like this.

Woof, woof, woof. What is going on? Champ barks along with me. Together we are loud, and Champ's man says, "No. Quiet Champ." Champ barks three more times before stopping. My girl comes over to me. She is smiling so everything must be okay. I wag and wiggle my happiness and am rewarded with a good bottom scratch.

"You picked that one up quickly," says Annette, as she walks over. "In a real situation, pull that leg up and lean back with everything you've got. Knees don't bend that way, and even if you don't break anything, the fucker won't be running after you any time soon."

Then she leans in and whispers. "I broke my ex's leg with that move, and he has never come around again."

When she pulls back, a wicked little smile crinkles the skin at the corner of her eyes. I give her a thumbs up.

"That's it for me," Annette says, and heads to the shoe wall. "I need to take a shower because I have a date tonight."

"I hope the poor dope knows what he's in for and minds his manners," Luca teases.

Annette laughs. With her shoes on and her purse over her shoulder, Annette walks towards Rae and me on her way out the door. She pauses to rub Rae's head.

"I'll see you two next week for the start of the Women Empowered workshop."

I smile and nod before giving her the thumbs up. Before I was dreading the class, but now I'm looking forward to it. I unwrap Rae's leash and walk her over to retrieve my shoes. Luca is giving Champ a good rub.

"You did good today. If you had pulled any harder, I might be hurting right now. Thanks for going easy on me," he says.

I curtsy, arms spread out as if to say, my pleasure, which of course it was.

The door opens and Rae rushes in past Sylvia.

"Hello to you, too," Sylvia says to the blur of black and white that makes a beeline inside to look for Frank.

I do a big open-hand wave and hug Sylvia before she closes the door behind me. For the last several months, we've been having dinner together on Sunday nights—a tradition started with my in-laws that feels like a lifetime ago. This, however, is a pleasure, whereas the in-laws Sunday gatherings felt like an obligation. I've offered to have Frank and Sylvia over to my small place, but Sylvia insisted I come here, saying she loves cooking for company. While I love to cook, as well, I do appreciate being a guest.

Where's the man? Where's the man? I don't see him or hear him. I smell where he has been, but he is not here. With my nose to the ground, I search him out. He is not in this big room. I run to the room with the good food smells. He is not in this room. Where is he? I bark at the lady. Maybe she knows where he is.

"Was that her way of asking where Frank is?" Sylvia asks. Then to Rae she says, "He's outside. Come on. I'll let you out."

The lady says words. I understand "come" and "out." I follow her. When she opens the door, I see him. The man with the treats. I race outside and bark before sitting at his feet. He is standing in front of a large metal thing that is hot. It smells like chicken. My nose is moving quickly to pull in the wonderful smells.

"Look who's come to dinner. The Rabbit Slayer. I'm guessing you want a treat, even though you haven't done any rabbit hunting today."

Treat. Treat. I put my paw on his leg. He points down. I lie down. I watch as he pulls the treat from his pocket. I take it gently from his hand. His hand smells of spices and chicken. I sprint away to eat my treat alone. "You're welcome!" *the man named Frank calls after me.*

Inside, Sylvia hands me a large ceramic platter and asks me to take it outside to Frank. As I walk out the door. Rae is chewing on something under the shade of a pine tree. When Frank and his treats are around, Rae ignores me.

"Hey, Lizzy."

I sign, "Hi, Dad."

I'm almost glad that I can't speak. It's hard for me to think of Frank as my father, let alone call him Dad. In my mind, I still think of him as Frank, the garden steward I met when I first moved to Pine City. Making the sign for "Dad" is somehow easier than saying the word. It's just a sign. No biggie. It does make him happy, though.

I don't have a sign I use for Sylvia, though. She is not my mother and doesn't want to be. If I could speak, I'd call her Sylvia. For now, I skip over calling her anything. I say, Hi. Bye. What have you been doing? None of which needs me to use her name.

"I found a recipe for jerk chicken. It might be a bit spicy.

Are you okay with spicy?" Frank asks.

I nod.

"I've put a plain piece aside for our little Rabbit Slayer. You can cut it up for her. I'm thinking about ten more minutes."

I give him the okay sign.

Sylvia joins us, handing Frank a cold beer. "What would you like? We have beer, red wine, sodas, or iced tea."

I point to Frank's beer and make the sign for "Thank you."

Frank uses a pair of tongs to turn over all the chicken breasts. As he takes a long draw on his beer, an ahhhh sound escapes his lips. Rae is back. Her paw rakes Frank's leg. Frank pulls out another piece of beef jerky.

"This is the last one." He snaps his fingers and Rae sits. He reaches down with an open hand and Rae lifts her paw to shake his hand. The last command, splayed fingers, elicits an enthusiastic bark. "Good girl," he says before handing Rae her treat, which she grabs before running back to the shade of the tree.

"She does love her treats," he says looking after her. Then turning to me he asks, "Are you ever going to tell us her real name?"

Frank would never harm Rae, but I'm hesitant. What if he shouts her name at the garden when other people are around? Then they will know her name and could call her. Rae is a friendly little girl. She'd probably run to anyone who calls her. She'd jump in their car, especially if they had a treat. She's not very discriminating. She's only eighteen months old, which according to new science makes her the equivalent of a fifteen-year-old teenager. Do I trust that she can discriminate between someone who is nice and someone who means to do her harm? No way.

To answer Frank, I mouth the word, "Someday."

"But not today," Frank concludes.

My shrug is an apology of sorts.

"I'll keep calling her Rabbit Slayer," he teases, knowing I hate the name.

My snarly look makes him laugh.

Frank spends the next few minutes filling me in on the drama at the community garden. While I'm the garden steward, Frank, thank god, still manages the gardeners. I don't know how he does it. The petty grievances sent via email alone drive me to drink. Not only is Frank my father, but he has the patience of a saint.

"Looks like these are ready," Frank says and begins transferring the chicken from the grill to the platter.

Frank carries the platter of cooked chicken breasts into the kitchen. Rae follows Frank as if he is the Pied Piper, the scent of barbeque acting like the piper's enticing music. I hold the door open for both of them. Sylvia has set the table including placing an iPad next to my plate so we can carry on a conversation. Salad, corn on the cob, and buttermilk rolls are already on the table. There is nothing left for me to do except sit. Rae makes herself at home by sitting under the table in case someone "accidentally" drops something.

Sylvia places a small bowl of water next to me. "For your dog."

"Thanks," I sign.

Dinner was delicious. The jerk chicken was spicy, but I loved it. There was enough left over that Sylvia put some in a container for me to take home. Rae loved her plain chicken as well. After wolfing down her food and receiving no more treats, she curled up on my feet for the remainder of the meal. Using the iPad propped up on a stand and a separate keyboard, I was able to carry on a conversation with short pauses. While I typed, they ate. Then while they read, I ate. In this way, we could carry on a semi-normal conversation. I told them I had something exciting to show them after dinner. So, after we cleaned up, we moved to the living room.

Now I switch to my cell phone to "talk." After a couple of visits, I figured out that we could use the screen-mirroring function on my phone and their television to display what I type on my phone. It works great. Sylvia loves it since she doesn't need her reading glasses.

Frank and Sylvia sit on the couch, facing the television, while Rae curls up on the couch next to Sylvia. At first, Sylvia didn't want Rae on the couch. But then Rae had placed her head on Sylvia's leg, focused her big puppy eyes on her, and whined sadly until Sylvia gave in. It didn't hurt that Rae doesn't shed. From then on, it was Sylvia who patted the couch for Rae.

Standing off to the side of the TV so they can watch what I'm typing, I begin. "Three weeks ago, I started taking a self-defense class. I want to show you what I've learned so far.

Frank, can you come here?"

"You're not going to throw me through the window, are you?"

I shake my head as Frank joins me. I have to pantomime what I want him to do. I point at Frank and then grab my wrist.

"You want me to grab you by the arm, right?"

I nod. I grab my arm again and hold it tight; shaking it to show him I want him to hold me tight. Frank grabs my arm above my wrist. He isn't holding me tightly. I clench my other fist.

"Tighter?"

I nod. When he has a good grip, I step forward, bending my elbow; pulling my fist toward my chest, and thrusting my elbow toward his, I pop out of his grasp.

"Wow," says Sylvia. "Were you holding her tight, Frank?"

"As tight as I could without bruising her," Frank says.

"Again," I mouth.

This time Frank grabs my arm with both hands. I feel the circulation being cut off to my fingers. Again, I break his hold.

"Impressive," Frank says.

Sylvia stands up, startling Rae. "I want to try."

Rae joins us, looking from Frank, to me, to Sylvia.

What are they doing? Is this a new game? I like games. I want to play. Woof. Woof.

Sylvia laughs. "Your dog is confused. I don't blame her. If someone were to look in the window, they would wonder what we are doing."

I motion Sylvia over and go through the steps slowly in the same fashion that Luca had taught me. Then I grab Sylvia's arm with one hand near her wrist. She breaks free.

"That was too easy. Frank. You hold me," she says, holding out her arm to Frank.

When she breaks free, her face lights up. "What else have you learned?"

We spend the next half hour going through various holds. I don't show her the leg grab that would have sent Frank to the floor, but I do demonstrate the "J" move for escaping a frontal throat grab.

"I hope you never need to use these moves, but I'm glad you know them," Frank says when we are all seated again. "Where's this class?"

Using the tablet, I tell them about the Jiu-Jitsu academy, Luca and Annette, and how next week Abby, her daughter Samantha, and I are starting the Women Empowered series.

"You should join us," I type and point to Sylvia.

"Me? I'd be the oldest person in the class," Sylvia protests, waving my suggestion away.

"Not true," I type. "There are women of all ages in the last class. It would be fun. Based on how quickly you picked up the moves tonight, you'd be good at this."

Sylvia beams at my compliment and then looks at Frank. "What do you think?"

"As long as you don't start throwing me around, I say go for it."

I clap my hands in excitement, which is Rae's signal to come, causing Rae to run to my side.

"Look. The dog wants to go, too. I'm feeling outnumbered," Frank jokes, although I do think he is feeling left out.

"I promise not to hurt you," Sylvia smirks. Then with a lifted eyebrow, "Unless that is something you would enjoy?"

Color rises from Frank's neck to his cheeks. "Let's take the Rabbit Slayer for a walk," he says, jumping up and heading for the door.

I wasn't the only one who felt uncomfortable with Sylvia's comment. Moments later, we are walking through their neighborhood, Frank and Sylvia holding hands while Rae and I follow behind. I have to admit I'm envious. I haven't held someone's hand like that in years. Charlie used to drape his arm over my shoulder as we walked along the beach or hold my hand when walking through town. I don't miss Charlie, but I do miss holding someone's hand. Suddenly, the remembered sensation of Luca pressed up against my back floods my senses. Rae stops, looks up at me, and barks.

Damn. How does she know?

Chapter Ten

Four Years Ago – September

During the week that I was cramping and expelling what the doctor called pregnancy tissue, Charlie was attentive, understanding, and just as sad as I was. And as Charlie had promised—because Charlie always keeps his promises—we found out the sex of our baby. A baby girl we named Claire. A month later, Charlie took me out on his longboard beyond the break. The setting sun was turning wisps of high clouds a golden orange as we bobbed on the gentle swells. We sat in silence, watching other surfers catch the slow, rolling waves, and ride them to shore. A squadron of pelicans cruised by in a line, their wingtips barely above the crest of a breaking wave. As the sun kissed the horizon, I gently placed a lei of white flowers onto the glistening water and watched as it floated away.

Wrapping my arms around Charlie and resting my head

against his strong back I whispered, "Farewell, my precious baby girl." I had never felt closer to him at that moment. It was a beautifully sad moment that I think of often.

A strange thing happened after we told Catherine the baby was a girl. She made this odd hmmph sound and then walked away. No big deal anymore since the baby wasn't the boy *she* wanted. I said as much to Charlie. He insisted that wasn't the case and that I should cut her some slack since *she* was grieving. But I know what I heard, how it sounded, and how she acted. She didn't care.

"Yes, she's fine," I heard Charlie say through the bathroom door, tipping me off that he was talking to his mother. "It's none of your business."

While two weeks before was the one-year anniversary of my miscarriage, the calls from Catherine started a mere three months after the loss of our baby. She used to call me directly … asking how I was feeling, had my body returned to normal? Then she would recite the latest information she'd dug up online on how second miscarriages are rare (which they are not), how it's best to keep trying (which we weren't), and how this time things would be different (how could she know). It made me want to scream, and sometimes I did … into my pillow, driving to work, on the deck with the crashing waves drowning out my anger. Since the miscarriage, my opinion of Catherine had deteriorated from an overbearing mother-in-law to a storybook villain such as Snow White and Cinderella's evil stepmothers.

"She's not ready." Pause. "I don't know. What's the rush?" Pause. "Jesus, Mom. You're not going to die." Long pause. "Okay, okay. I'll ask her."

When I walked out of the bathroom, Charlie was sitting on the edge of the bed looking out the window at the ocean. He turned to speak, and I cut him off before he could say a word.

"Don't. I'm not ready."

"I know, I know. But when do you think you *will* be ready? I need to tell her something. She's driving me crazy," Charlie pleaded.

"I'll be ready when I'm ready," I said turning away from him.

My excuses were lined up. I didn't want to conceive in January and be huge during the summer. May was out because that was when we conceived last time. I was too hot and grumpy in June and July, and August was out of the question because that was when I miscarried.

At thirty-four, my biological clock's tick-tock was more like church bells ringing in the distance instead of an alarm clock blaring. Apparently, Catherine's clock was speeding up, since she told Charlie that she would be dead before we finally conceived and delivered her a grandson. Then she had the nerve to tell me that if I wanted more than one kid we needed to "giddy up." The nerve of that woman made me want to break something.

She had no idea what I was going through. I found myself crying when I saw a pregnant woman, or a small baby—and they were everywhere. Returning to work at the hospital, I went to great lengths to avoid the maternity ward, mostly by hunkering down in the kitchen and never leaving.

Charlie, on the other hand, recovered more quickly from the experience, returning to surfing, and showing up at his family's corporate board meetings a week later. It was different for me. As my breasts shrunk back to their normal size, and my periods returned, I missed being pregnant. I didn't miss the nausea or the odd aches, but I felt empty. I caught myself protectively placing a hand on my belly or looking sideways in a mirror to catch a hint of my baby bump. One time, when I had indigestion, for a nanosecond, I caught myself thinking, "Oh! The baby moved." Then I'd burst into tears. I tried to keep this from Charlie because he had moved on and didn't understand why I hadn't.

It was three weeks before Charlie's birthday when Catherine called. She wanted to take us out to dinner at this new exclusive restaurant—they would pay she reassured me—to celebrate Charlie's big day. Of course, she had to remind me that we hadn't celebrated his birthday last year because I was too depressed over the baby. Nice one. After I agreed, the conversation changed.

"You know what Charlie would like for his birthday, don't you?" Catherine asked.

"I do. I'm buying him a new wetsuit. But please don't tell him."

"I'm sure he'll love it, but that's not what I'm suggesting … if you catch my meaning."

Silence.

Really? My mother-in-law was telling me to have birthday sex with her son? I wish I was using an old-fashioned handset so I could slam the receiver or throw the phone against the wall.

Instead, I took a deep breath. In the most cheerful voice I could muster, I said, "Ohhhh. I understand. You don't have to worry, Catherine. I always give your little boy a nice, long, blowjob on his birthday."

Her gasp of shock was very satisfying. I tapped the red button and disconnected the call.

Sitting on the balcony enjoying the scenery, reading, and sipping on an iced coffee I'd picked up on the way home, I was trying to unwind from a hectic day at work. The hospital had lost one of its cooks and the new chef wasn't all we hoped she would be. I'd spent more time in the kitchen today than usual, trying to bring Ms. Natalie up to speed. Not my job, but someone had to do it. Reading kept me from thinking about the job and immersed me in someone else's problems.

Two chapters into my mystery novel, the guy I pegged as the murderer stood outside the heroine's apartment, staring up at her window. The scene was all dark-and-stormy night-ish and had me on edge. So, when a loud bang, crash, and the sound of breaking glass came from the garage, I practically jumped out of my skin.

Walking through the house, and down the hallway, the noise level continued to build. It sounded like someone was trashing the garage. I tiptoed the last few feet and quickly turned the deadbolt to keep the crazy person in the garage from coming into the house. As I lifted my phone to call the police, I heard Charlie's voice.

"God fucking damn you!" Then something hit a wall.

Jesus. Is Charlie in there fighting off a burglar? I pounded on the door. "Charlie, are you alright? I'm calling the police right now."

"No!" he shouted. "Don't call the police. I'm fine."

He tried opening the door. "Hey. Unlock the door. It's fine. Just an accident."

I quickly unlocked the door and there stood Charlie. He was out of breath, covered in sweat, and hunched over with his hands on his knees as if he'd run a marathon. Looking over his shoulders, a war zone spread out behind him. There were aluminum beach chairs in a tangled heap. Sports equipment that used to hang neatly on the wall was scattered everywhere. The shelving system that held extra pantry items leaned on Charlie's car with bags of potato chips, paper towels, and toilet paper scattered everywhere.

My hands went to my mouth. "What happened? Are you okay?"

Slowly, Charlie stood straighter and looked around as if

noticing the mess for the first time.

"Oh, geez," he said, shaking his head as if waking up from a bad dream.

"Seriously, what happened? Were you attacked? I heard you shouting at someone."

Charlie looked down at his hand and then around the garage. I followed his gaze. Lying on the floor in front of my car was Charlie's cell phone. Looking like his legs were made of concrete, he retrieved his phone. He turned the screen toward me. The glass was shattered.

"Looks like I'll be buying a new phone. I needed an upgrade anyway," he said with a hiccupping laugh. "I need a drink."

He pushed past me leaving me standing in the doorway surveying the disaster. Six holes were punched into the drywall, and a baseball bat—the likely culprit—was discarded on the floor. Hmmm. How would he explain that?

After he downed two tumblers of scotch, he told me what had happened. When he drove into the garage he'd been on the phone, distracted, and didn't stop in time. He hit the bottom of the shelving system, which tipped over sending everything flying. When he tried to stand the shelf back up, he hadn't realized that all the sports equipment was connected to the shelves as well, and as he struggled, more stuff came flying off the wall. When the chairs hit him in the head, he'd flung them away as a reaction to being "attacked."

He didn't say anything about the baseball bat, the holes in the drywall, or his shattered phone. I had a pretty good idea who he'd been talking to and decided not to open that can of smelly worms.

At seven, I was already in the kitchen making Charlie's favorite breakfast for his birthday—blueberry pancakes, lots of syrup, and sausage. A bottle of champagne with two glasses sat next to the carton of orange juice for mimosas. I'd placed the wetsuit inside a box, inside a box, inside a box, so that Charlie would have to unwrap three boxes before he got to his present. The box took up the majority of the glass kitchen table.

Charlie wandered in wearing the blue bathrobe his mother had given him for his birthday the night we went out for dinner. I growled internally, although I knew he'd like the wetsuit more than her stupid bathrobe.

Charlie squinted at the bright light coming through the wall of windows. "Coffee," he said, arms outstretched like he was Frankenstein.

"We're having mimosas," I said, pointing to the bottle of champagne.

"I need coffee first."

He wasn't excited about the mimosas and hadn't noticed the enormous, wrapped present on the table.

"I'm making your favorite breakfast," I tried. "Happy birthday."

"Oh, right? I forgot," he said, coming over and putting his arms around my waist. Then reaching around me, he took a cooked sausage.

"Hey," I protested.

He just laughed. "Babe, you know I hate to wait."

When breakfast was ready, he gobbled down his food like he was in an eating contest. "What's this?" he asked, finally acknowledging the box.

"It's your birthday present!" I was more excited than he was.

His expression changed. It was like a cloud had passed in front of the sun. His mouth stretched into a flat line. "Really. I find that odd."

"Odd?" Every nerve vibrated a warning as the space between us crackled with tension.

"A little birdie told me I would be getting a blowjob for my birthday, and I'm wondering how that can be inside this box."

My face flushed. Catherine.

Turning in his seat to face me, Charlie untied the belt around his bathrobe, pulling it open; his erection was obvious. "I'm ready for my present."

He grabbed my hand, pulled me out of my chair then pushed me down on my knees. With two hands on my head, he tried to force my head into his lap. Planting my hands on either side of the chair, I pushed myself up and away.

"I don't want to do this now. I'm going to be late for work."

"But it's my birthday and you told my mother you were going to give me a blowjob, so give me a blowjob."

"I can't believe your mother told you that," I said, backing away until my back was pressed against the cold steel of the refrigerator door.

Charlie stood. He didn't close his robe. "I can't believe YOU told my mother that. She was so upset. Remember when I crashed my car into the garage? That was because my mother was telling me what a little slut you are and how you were going to give me a blowjob."

I shook my head.

"You're right. I can't make you. But look at me. I'm ready. I've waited long enough to make a baby. Let's do this," he said, taking my hand. "It's my birthday. It's time to give me my present."

His dark eyes were hard, and his mouth was set in a sneer as he pulled me from the kitchen toward the couch. I grabbed at the counter, but he jerked my arm, and I lost my grip.

"Stop it, Charlie. You're scaring me."

The next thing I knew, he had pushed me onto the couch and was climbing on top of me. I screamed for him to stop, but this only infuriated him more. As he ripped off my panties, I turned my head away, closed my eyes, and imagined I was on a boat, the ocean waves lapping against the hull.

Chapter Eleven

Clap, Clap, Clap – Come

Samantha, Abby's daughter, holds the door open for her mother, Sylvia, and me as we exit the Jiu-Jitsu academy. Rae walks beside me on her leash, and Samantha catches up, giving Rae a good bottom scratch, which has Rae spinning in circles of appreciation.

"That class was sick. I can't wait to practice those moves on Dylan," Samantha says as she pulls her light brown hair out of her ponytail.

"Only if you promise not to hurt him." Abby gives her daughter a look that I'm guessing means she knows Samantha would like to throw her brother over her shoulder.

Samantha rolls her eyes and runs to their car. With her hair around her face, she looks like Abby's Mini Me. By the time Abby and I are exchanging hugs and saying goodbye, Samantha has her earbuds in, disconnecting her from the real world.

I walk over to Sylvia's car as she's climbing inside.

"That was a good class. I'm going to make your father practice with me tonight. I'll retain the information better if I practice as soon as possible. How do you practice?" she asks.

I go through the motions of escaping a front stranglehold, followed by an escape from a two-handed grab.

"By yourself?"

I nod.

"I'll have Frank practice with you on Sunday. I'm trying a new recipe, Fettuccine Alfredo with roasted vegetables. Frank keeps bringing vegetables home from the community garden. It's difficult finding new ways to cook zucchini. Thank God for the internet."

Rubbing my hands together to signal anticipation, I mouth the word "yummy."

"Come a little early so we can practice. Frank will complain, but he'll love it." Sylvia waves goodbye before pulling out of the parking lot.

Back at my car, I let Rae in first and am about to climb in when I hear someone calling my name. Luca and Champ are heading my way. As bold as can be, Champ pushes past me and jumps into my car. Rae is sitting in the passenger seat, and Champ takes his place in the driver's seat. I look from Champ back to Luca shaking my head and throwing my hands in the air as if to say, "What the hell?"

"Champ. Come," Luca tries, but Champ lays down, his head on Rae's paws.

Rae lays down as well, placing her head on Champ.

Luca takes one look at the two dogs and lets out a booming laugh. His laugh is as deep as the ocean and as rich as dark chocolate. It's the first time I've heard him laugh and it makes me feel warm all over like a snifter of brandy on a winter night.

"Champ," he tries again with no effect. "They like each other."

Looking inside I have to admit they do look pretty cute together. This is Rae's first four-legged friend. We don't go to dog parks. I don't have friends with dogs. I am her pack, and she is mine. Looking at her now with her head resting on Champ's head, I feel a little bad for keeping her from having a dog friend. For the last few weeks, whenever I come to class, I've hooked Rae's leash to the bench and then stepped onto the mat without looking back. But at the end of class, there is Champ, curled up next to Rae. They are an item.

I like Champ. I want him to come home with me. His man keeps calling him. Champ stays with me. The man reaches in and grabs Champ's collar. He pulls him away from me. Woof. I want Champ to stay. Champ is pulled out of the car. I follow him out of the car. Together we run back to the building where we can be together. We sit at the door. We wait for the door to open so we can go inside but it doesn't open.

"Champ has never acted like this before," says Luca with remnants of his laugh still coloring his words.

I pull out my phone so I can communicate with more than shrugs and signs. I type, "Except for a quick sniff on our neighborhood walks, Rae hasn't been around other dogs." But before I turn the phone around to Luca, I catch myself. I change Rae to "She" and then show Luca.

"What are we going to do? They obviously like each other," Luca says as he stares at the two dogs sitting patiently by the door.

"They do," I type.

"It would be nice ... for them ... if they could spend more time together. Maybe we could go on a hike or a walk ... for the sake of the dogs? I could show you some of our favorite trails."

Typing ... "My dog would enjoy a hike. We haven't ventured out except for walks around our neighborhood." I show Luca the screen.

"Great. Would you prefer a hike with a view or something amongst the trees?"

Hmmm. I know several trails venture up into the mountains. Up until now, I haven't been willing to hike alone, especially for the first year when she was a puppy. It's not safe. I've heard of coyotes attacking dogs on the trails not to mention rattlesnakes and even the occasional bear. And while all of that is true, what I've been more afraid of is the human factor. Men, to be specific, but this could be okay. I'll have two dogs and a black belt

Jiu-Jitsu instructor, who despite his ability to toss men through the air as if they weigh nothing, comes across as caring and respectful.

"I love the reward of a great view after trudging up a hill," I type.

Luca moves in closer to read what I've written. I can't help the memory that sneaks up on me of Charlie leaning in close to kiss me on the cheek after a day of surfing. Charlie smelled of salt water. Luca smells like a pleasing mix of musk, wood smoke, and dog. I slowly inhale deeper, making sure Luca is unaware of what I'm doing, and catch a hint of eucalyptus and peppermint in his hair ... probably his shampoo. I type more so he stays close.

"I've heard there is a trail that has views of the desert below. Do you know that one? I'm looking for something uncrowded so I can take my dog off-leash. Do you take Champ off leash?"

Luca finishes reading and steps back. Dang. It was good while it lasted. It's been so long since I've been that close to a man, except for the fleeting moments in class. The way my body is reacting, I miss it more than I realize.

"I have the perfect spot. And yes, I do let Champ off-leash. If we go early in the morning, there won't be any people. The trail is on the east end of the Valley. When do you want to go?"

"Saturday?" I mouth, using my hands to indicate a question.

"Sure. Let's meet here at nine. You can follow me in your car to the trailhead."

He must have guessed that I wouldn't have been comfortable driving together. I give him points for understanding. I like Luca, but I don't know him beyond class. I doubt he would try anything since I could ruin his reputation. A teacher of self-defense for women, attacks a woman? However, just to be safe, I'll tell Abby where I'm going and who I'm going with, even though I'll have to answer to her version of the Spanish Inquisition.

I give Luca the okay sign and hold up nine fingers to indicate I understand what time to meet.

"Bring water for yourself and your dog. Do you have a collapsible bowl?"

I shake my head.

"If you can pick one up, that would be great. If not, she can share Champ's bowl."

Looks like I'll be visiting the pet store before Saturday. I clap three times for Rae to come. She looks at me and doesn't move. I clap three more times and slide into the driver's seat. Rae's fear of being left behind overrides her desire to stay with Champ, and she charges across the parking lot. She doesn't slow down when she reaches the open door and leaps across me onto the passenger seat.

Luca steps up and closes the door for me. "See you Saturday."

I nod and make the okay sign. Thinking of Saturday, I suddenly feel giddy like a teenager anticipating the prom.

I didn't sleep well Friday night in anticipation of my date-that's-not-a-date with Luca. I called Abby in the evening, which I'm thinking was a mistake, as she morphed into a giggly girl with a dozen questions and theories: "What if he wants to hold your hand? What if he tries to kiss you? Is the whole dog thing a ploy? He wanted to ask you out but didn't know how. He's using his dog as his wingman. What if he doesn't try and kiss you? Will you make the first move?"

All her questions filled my mind with concerns of my own. I'd started a text calling the whole thing off when Abby called and said, "You better go. No chickening out."

So here I am, sitting in the parking lot with a new day pack filled with water bottles, a collapsible dog bowl, my cell phone, and a granola bar. I'm wearing a pair of hiking boots that I bought when I moved to the mountains but have never used. Online research touted the benefits of dressing in layers, which explains my outfit –a tank top, covered by a long-sleeve shirt, covered by a windbreaker. A ball cap, sunglasses, and sunscreen offer protection from the sun.

Physically, I'm ready. Mentally, I'm a mess. Second thoughts have me starting the car and shifting into reverse just as Luca pulls up next to me. I could say I'm not feeling well, which wouldn't be a total lie. My stomach is doing flip-flops, and even though it's not hot yet, I break out in a sweat that has me wiping my brow. Rae sees Champ and jumps into my lap to stick her head out the window. When she barks a hello, I jump out of my skin.

Chill out. It's just a hike … for the dogs. But like Abby, I don't think this is about bringing these star-crossed doggies together. Rae starts whining as Luca and Champ walk over. Holding Rae so she doesn't jump out the window, I'm still coming up with excuses for canceling.

"Hey. Ready to hike?"

Excuses fade when I look at Luca's open smile. I nod, hoping the smile I flash him hides the anxiety I'm feeling.

"Great. Follow me. We'll head out to the east valley on Pine City Boulevard. We'll drive into the hills through a residential neighborhood to the trailhead. It's a local's trail that cuts up the mountain to this famous rock outcropping. It's pretty impressive and has a great view of the valley. Then we can walk over to the Pacific Crest Trail and hike that for a bit. That's where we can find the desert views. How does that sound?"

I make the okay sign but then point to my watch.

Luca doesn't understand, so I pick up my phone and ask, "How long will we be gone?"

"Oh. Two hours unless you have to be somewhere."

I shake my head and give another okay sign. As Luca is walking back to his car, I text Abby. "We are going to a hiking trail in the east valley to check out this "impressive" rock and then along the PCT. Luca says two hours. If you don't hear from me by noon, call the police." Then in case she doesn't know I'm kidding, I add, "Just kidding, but I will call you when I'm back."

Luca parks his white Jeep on a dirt road that dead ends at the edge of a pinon pine forest. There are houses scattered up and down the road but no traffic or people. Perfect.

The delineation between forest and private property is created by a four-foot-tall wood and wire fence. When I open the car door, Rae leaps over my lap and hits the dirt running. She has a bad case of the zoomies and is kicking up a cloud of dust as she runs in large circles up and down the street. I'd be worried that she's not on a leash but there is no one around. She doesn't stop until Luca opens his door and Champ jumps out. Champ acts like he missed his morning coffee as he ambles over to the closest tree and lifts his leg. Rae is intrigued by this and sticks her nose under Champ's leg. I want to yell, "No!" Instead, I clap and stomp, but the stomp on the dirt barely makes a sound and does nothing to dissuade Rae.

"It's already warming up," Luca says as he pulls his sweatshirt over his head to reveal a pale green t-shirt with a hiking sloth complete with hiking shoes, a backpack, and a walking stick.

As he's stuffing his sweatshirt into his day pack, I can finally read the words on his shirt. "Sloth Hiking Team. We get there when we get there." I snort my version of a laugh and Luca looks up.

"What?"

I try an easy sign language sentence. First, I point at myself. Then I make the sign for like … flat hand to the chest, then touching the thumb and the middle finger I pull my hand away.

Then I point at Luca's t-shirt. As I do this, I mouth the words, I like your shirt.

"You like me?"

Too quickly, I shake my head.

Luca cocks his head. "You don't like me?"

Again, I shake my head, a bit embarrassed. I step closer and try again, but this time instead of pointing at him, I grab a handful of his t-shirt.

"Ohhhhh. You like my t-shirt," he laughs, then continues. "My hikes are leisurely … sloth-like. It's not a race. I want to enjoy the scenery."

I nod, smile, and give him a thumbs up, hoping he understands.

Day pack on, phone in hand, I follow Luca to an opening in the fence that indicates the start of the trail. The trail is only one person wide, so we walk single file, Champ and Rae leading the way and Luca bringing up the rear. The dogs are walking/running twice as far since they run ahead, stop, run back to us, then run ahead again. Each time Champ and Rae come back, Luca pulls out two small treats, ensuring they will always come back. I nod my approval. Luca hands me several treats and wants me to call Rae.

Putting the treats in my pocket, I clap my hands three times. Rae stops and looks back over her shoulder. I clap three times again, then pull out a treat. Now she sprints back, sits, and barks. She grabs the treat and takes off up the trail to rejoin Champ.

"When I first started taking Champ hiking, I always brought treats. Just these small kibble things but it was a way of rewarding him for coming when I called. Now he comes back and checks on me without the treats, but I thought I'd bring them for your dog."

I mouth, "Thanks."

Besides the three hand claps, I also have my dog whistle on a chain tucked inside my shirt. When the dogs are around a corner and out of sight, I pull out the whistle and give it a try. Both dogs come rushing back and are rewarded with treats. Rae can't pinpoint where sounds are coming from because of her bad ear. When we were training with the dog whistle in the backyard, she could see me. This is the first time she's been out of my sight when I've used the whistle. I'm happy that she was able to come back and find me, although having Champ and a trail to follow was a big help.

Talking as we hike isn't easy, so after a few general comments, we hike in silence making it easier to hear the sounds of the forest: the breeze sweeping through the upper branches of the pines; the call of a Pinon Jay as it glides, wings spread wide, between trees; the high-pitch buzz of cicadas that sounds like electricity; and the crunch of rocks under our feet.

The trail switchbacks up the mountain, crossing a dry creek four times until we break free of the trees into an open area. The trail splits off to the left and right. Both dogs are sitting at the junction, pink tongues lolling out of the sides of their mouths.

"We're going to the right," Luca says, pointing in that direction.

Champ understands and follows the trail to the right. Rae waits for me.

"It's not that much further. We can enjoy the view and give the dogs water."

Moments later, a huge outcropping of white rock comes into view. As big as a school bus, I don't know if the rock forced its way out of the ground or the ground eroded around it. Champ climbs up the smooth rocks and finds a cool slab where he lies down. The ground around the solid rock dome is littered with pieces of white stone. I grab one for a closer look.

"It's quartz. Not the clear crystal version, but still quartz. This place is sacred to the native people who call it Hatauva. It's part of their creation story. Locals call it the *Eye of God*."

I climb up the steep rocks and find a flat area where I can sit. Rae follows and leans against my leg. Looking west, we have an unobstructed view of the valley below encircled by tree-covered mountains. Definitely worth the uphill hike. I fill Rae's new water bowl and then take a long drink myself before refilling her now empty bowl.

Luca doesn't sit next to me but finds a flat rock next to Champ. He doesn't speak and we all enjoy the view, lost in our thoughts.

Tired. Tired, tired, tired. I want to stay here. I lift my nose to the breeze. New scents come my way. I can smell Champ and his man. I can smell the pine trees and the smell of rotting wood. Coming from down below are smells of other dogs and the wild dogs that yip and howl at night. I like this place. I can smell so much without moving.

I click a few pictures of the view. Mom would probably like a photo of Rae and me, so I carefully climb over the smooth surface of the rocks to Luca. I tap him on the shoulder, startling him out of his trance-like meditation. I show him my phone and pantomime taking a picture.

Rae and I stand on the highest point of the quartz dome, our backs to the view. Luca has positioned himself to take it all in. I motion that we should switch places so I can take his picture with Champ, but he shakes off my offer. Instead, he suggests we take a picture of the two dogs. Using treats to capture their attention, we snap a great image of the two doggie friends, standing tall and proud on top of the white rock with the view behind them.

Photo shoot complete, Luca pulls out cheese, crackers, almonds, and some grapes from his pack and lays them out on a paper plate like a poor man's charcuterie.

Bummer. No wine. But who am I to complain? My contribution is a single granola bar, which I unwrap, break in half, and set on the plate.

We don't hike much farther after the stop at the Eye of God. Rae is dragging and I am worried I'll have to carry her back. Apparently, I've raised a pretty, pretty princess who prefers sleeping all day to rigorous adventures along mountain trails. We do walk over to a section of the Pacific Crest Trail, so I'm rewarded with a view of the desert below but then head back. There is never a suggestion from either of us to take any selfies. At first, I am relieved, but later I'm disappointed. Maybe this *is* only about the dogs after all.

Back at the house, Rae crashes on the couch, and I call Abby.

There is no preamble when Abby picks up the phone. "So? What happened? Was it great? Did sparks fly?"

Texting ... "It was a nice hike. We went to this place called The Eye of God. Luca brought snacks, the dogs enjoyed themselves, then I drove home."

"The dogs enjoyed themselves. Well, I'm glad to hear that," Abby says, sarcasm dripping off the word "dogs."

More typing. "I had a nice time, as well, but I do think Luca was just being nice. He wasn't interested in me at all. He practically fell asleep when we were gazing out at the view. It wasn't a date disguised as a hike with the dogs. It was a hike with the dogs."

It's times like these that I'm glad I can't speak since Abby would have heard the disappointment in my voice.

"That's a bummer. Would you want to go hiking again ... if he asks?"

I sigh.

"I heard that. You were disappointed, weren't you?"

My thumbs move quickly to reply. "A little. But I'm sure

it's for the best. He is my instructor. It might feel weird in class if we were dating."

"You're adults. You'd figure it out. Hey, I gotta run. The kids are into it again. Call me if anything changes. Promise?"

I send her a smiley face before setting the phone down. In the kitchen, I make myself a small salad and pour a glass of wine. I'm not normally a day drinker, but what the heck? Maybe a glass of wine will take the edge off my disappointment. After a few bites and sips, I look at my phone to find a new text. This one is from Luca.

"I enjoyed our hike today. But I'm thinking that hiking probably wasn't the best way to be able to talk to you since it's hard to hike and type. Would you be up for dinner sometime? There's this great outdoor place where we can bring the dogs."

Staring at the words on the screen, those four sentences convey so much. It wasn't all about the dogs after all. Jumping up, I do a butt-wiggling happy dance of my own. Rae looks at me like I've lost it. She might be right.

Chapter Twelve

Four Years Ago – December

I remember praying for my period to start once before when I was eighteen. That time, I'd only been a couple of days late. But this time, all the prayers in the world had not changed the fact that I was pregnant. My body was already gearing up for the big event, although no nausea this time. On one hand, I was happy to be pregnant again, but on the other, I still had residual anger over how it had happened. Charlie apologized the next day saying he didn't know what had come over him. He described it as a blinding storm of rage over which he had no control.

For someone who is usually mellow and laid back, his fits of anger (and I'd seen a few) were like a person possessed by a demon. Up until Charlie's birthday, his "fits" have never been directed at me.

When it came to this pregnancy, I planned to wait as long

as possible before telling Charlie. I wasn't ready to be thrust into the spotlight once again. I imagined it would be even worse this time around. If Catherine treated me like a porcelain doll before, I fully expected to be bound up in bubble wrap the moment she found out. The plan was working until my very observant husband called me out.

"There haven't been any of your little packages in the bathroom trash in some time. When was your last period?" he asked as we sat on the floor wrapping Christmas gifts.

Imagining him checking the trash before he takes it out gave me a chill as if a dark cloud passed in front of the sun. Trying to sound casual, I said, "Hmm. I don't know. I'd have to look at my calendar."

Charlie stopped ... A length of tape suspended over a package. "Go look, then."

"It's on my phone. I can look after we're done."

"Where's your phone?"

I shrugged. "Probably upstairs on the nightstand. Or maybe in my purse. I'm not sure."

Charlie finished taping up the package he was working on and tossed it my way. "It's ready for the bow." Then he stood and headed upstairs. When he returned, he had my phone in his hand. "What's your passcode?"

Instead of answering him, I held out my hand. Moments later, looking at my calendar, I admitted I hadn't had a period since before his birthday.

"When were you going to tell me?" Charlie wanted to know, irritation making his voice sharp.

"I wanted to be sure. Then I was going to surprise you."

"You're not sure?"

Running a knife along the edge of a ribbon made a vibrating sound like a zipper being opened. The sound made me shiver as if the knife was sliding across my raw emotions. I secured the curly ribbon to a package, needing a moment before I answered.

"I haven't been to the doctor or taken a pregnancy test. So, no, I'm not sure."

Again, Charlie headed up the stairs and when he returned, he had a home pregnancy test. Without saying a word, he held the box out to me.

Setting aside the scissors, I took the box. Dread was making these simple movements painfully slow as if I were moving through pudding. "You want me to do this now?"

Charlie nodded before sitting on the floor cross-legged. He picked up the next box in the pile, measuring paper, and cutting the length he needed.

Resigned, I headed to the bathroom. Sitting on the toilet, head in my hands, I knew what the result was going to be. What I didn't know was how Charlie was going to react. Would he be angry that I hadn't told him, or would his happiness overshadow that fact?

After flushing the toilet and washing my hands, I sat there

staring at the two small openings in the plastic tester. First, one blue line appeared … then a second blue line. I was pregnant. Charlie knocked on the door.

"Are you okay in there?"

An excellent question. Was I okay? I didn't know the answer to that question, so I stood and opened the door, thrusting the stick at him.

He looked down at the results and then up at me. "We're having a baby," he whooped, before picking me up and spinning me around.

Driving up to the Bouchard mansion on Christmas day I felt like Alice stepping through the looking glass. The driveway maze was outlined in small white lights creating a striking pattern, while evenly spaced flocked pine trees marched like good little soldiers to the main entry. Standing as sentries on either side of the massive front door were two, twenty-foot-tall pines, also flocked, but these trees had glowing red lights that turned the white flocking red. This did nothing to vanquish the illusion that I was entering Wonderland to meet the Queen of Hearts.

Charlie's arms were filled with gifts as were mine, so Charlie kicked the front door instead of ringing the bell. As if he had been standing on the other side awaiting our arrival, Mac opened the door before the echo of Charlie's kick faded.

"Master Bouchard. Ms. Bouchard. Merry Christmas," Mac said, not sounding the least bit merry as he held the door open.

"You can take the gifts into the grand parlor. Your mother and father are waiting there. What can I bring you to drink?"

"Champagne," Charlie said with a little too much glee.

Mac nodded and looked at me. "Tea to start," which elicited a raised eyebrow. Maybe I was the first person to request Catherine's god-awful tea.

"Bring the whole bottle, will you? We're celebrating," Charlie added.

My eyes burned with a warning that Charlie ignored. For days, we'd been going around and around about when to tell Catherine I was pregnant. I wanted to wait until after the New Year. Charlie wanted to tell his mother the moment we found out. I was just over eleven weeks along; twelve weeks on the 28th. We had an appointment on January 5th that would include an ultrasound and the confirmation of a fetal heartbeat. I wanted to wait until after that, just to make sure the baby was doing well before we told anyone, especially Catherine.

We walked down the hallway in the glow of a thousand red twinkle lights adorning a dozen living trees in red pots. When we entered the grand parlor, I gasped.

"Wow," said Charlie. "You've outdone yourself this year, Mother."

Catherine rose from her throne to greet us looking regal as always. Her red velvet knee-length dress draped elegantly over black tights and knee-high black boots screamed "Queen of Hearts." I could have sworn I heard the command, "Off with her head!" hidden within the lyrics of the holiday music and a chill rushed up my spine and settled at the base of my neck.

I wasn't sure if Charlie honestly loved the decorations or if he was simply pandering to his mother. Martha Stewart on steroids was my first impression. The place glowed like a nuclear disaster. From the three trees covered top to bottom with nothing but white lights, to the deep green pine garland that framed each window and the door. From the half dozen three-foot-tall glass vases filled with tiny red fairy lights, to the warmer glow of several dozen candles in silver candle holders lined up across the top of the mantle, the room was so full of light I was tempted to whip out my sunglasses.

"Here," Catherine said, pointing to the middle tree. "Place your gifts under the tree."

With packages under the largest of the three trees, our arms were now free to give Catherine the required hug, which she accepted stiffly. Before we could hand out more of the expected compliments, Charlie's father burst into the room saving the day, a glass of dark amber in his hand.

"Hooray. You're here. Now can we turn the goddamn lights down? I feel like I'm on a stage," my father-in-law said in a booming voice, signaling that the drink he now finished off had been half empty, not half full.

Catherine shook her head in disgust. "Fine." She strolled over to a switch on the wall, and I watched in relief as all the lights, except the candles, dimmed to a tolerable glow.

"It's lovely," I was finally able to say truthfully. "I

especially love the candles."

Catherine acknowledged my comment with a slight tip of her head and a smile before giving her husband the stink eye, which didn't faze him in the least. Mac walked in and handed Charlie a glass of champagne, then placed a silver bucket with the bottle on the table with three additional flutes.

"Are we celebrating something?" Catherine asked, inspecting my body for signs I might be pregnant.

I was wearing a pair of thick, waist-high yoga pants that were doing an excellent job of flattening my baby bump. A tight bra that compressed my swollen breasts and an oversized holiday sweater completed my disguise.

"Nah. Just happy to be here and drinking your exquisite champagne," Charlie replied, lifting his flute in a toast.

"I'm happy you are here as well," Charlie's father said, pouring champagne into his now-empty cocktail glass.

"Robert Michael Bouchard! We do not drink Dom Pérignon from a tumbler," Catherine said as she walked over to him.

Charlie's dad must have known what was coming since he turned away and downed his champagne before Catherine could snatch his glass away. Turning back, he handed her the tumbler. Catherine shook her head and rolled her eyes.

"Such a child." Then to Mac, "Bring Mr. Bouchard a flute of champagne."

Catherine motioned to the beautiful but very uncomfortable

couch where she wanted us to sit. Moments later, Mac brought in the silver tea service and a pot of Catherine's imported tea, setting it on the antique table in front of us.

"Tea?" Catherine asked, looking me up and down again, suspicion making her eyes narrow.

I was ready for her, though. "I just loved the tea you served the first time we met. I haven't had anything like it since. I hope you don't mind if I start the evening with a cup instead of something stronger."

Catherine glowed almost as brightly as her candles at my compliment. "I'm so pleased you like it. Next time I order some, I'll buy you a small packet as well."

"That would be wonderful," I lied.

Her tea was harsh and needed copious amounts of sugar to make it drinkable, even though I was only allowed one cube.

"May I?" Mac inquired, indicating that he would pour me a cup.

I nodded.

"Sugar?"

"Yes, please. One lump."

Catherine smiled her approval, then turned her attention to Charlie. That's when I caught Mac adding four lumps of sugar. He looked at me and winked before straightening up and bowing slightly before leaving the room.

Looks like I have an ally. Picking up my teacup, I stirred the sugar cubes until they dissolved. Catherine's full attention was on her son so I was able to sneak another sugar cube into her god-awful tea. I sat back and tried to get comfortable while Catherine quizzed her son about his role on the board, asking if he was ready to be more involved in their foundation, and various other family businesses. Charlie's father sat next to me and lifted his flute in a salute before emptying the entire glass in one gulp. Then he burped. I was so surprised that a giggle escaped my lips.

Catherine whipped her head around and glared at her husband. "Disgusting," she pronounced before turning back to Charlie.

Mr. Bouchard shrugged. He leaned in and whispered to me, "It's the bubbles. It happens all the time."

Smiling I asked, "What have you been up to, Mr. Bouchard?"

"Robert. Call me Robert, please."

"Okay, Robert. What have you been doing lately."

"This and that. Although I did have a good round of golf last Thursday. Three pars and several bogeys, and I didn't lose a single ball. Do you golf?" Robert asked, perking up.

"Afraid not. I'm not very athletic."

The excitement left his eyes as he realized I wasn't a golfer. Luckily Mac came in at that moment and announced dinner was served. Robert perked up again, reached over, and squeezed my knee.

"This is my favorite meal of the year. You think Catherine goes all out with the decorations, wait until dinner. She's serving a real Christmas goose!"

Three hours later, dinner was over, the gifts had been opened, and Mac was bringing in snifters of cognac. I took mine and simply inhaled. That alone was enough to make my head feel light. I'd had two sips of red wine at dinner just to keep Catherine's suspicions at bay. Several times I raised the glass to my lips but didn't drink. As I raised the snifter, Charlie shook his head. I let the warm liquid touch my lips before setting the glass on the table. I made sure no one was looking before sticking out my tongue at Charlie who rolled his eyes at my childish response.

Charlie and Catherine were two peas in a pod. They had the same eye rolls, the same tendency to snatch drinks away from their spouses, and the same condescending looks, although, in this situation, I knew Charlie was motivated by his concern for the baby.

After a healthy sip of cognac, Charlie stood and went to the tree. Bending down and reaching back, he pulled out another package.

"Hey, look. We forgot one," he said, walking over to Catherine.

He handed her a royal blue bracelet box tied with a silver ribbon. I didn't remember wrapping that gift or Charlie telling me he'd bought his mother a bracelet.

"Oh, Charlie. You didn't have to buy me a new bangle," she said, but her eyes said she was delighted.

She pulled the ribbon off and then opened the hinged lid. While I couldn't see the bracelet, there was something about it that caused a moment of stunned silence. That must be some bracelet to render Catherine speechless. How could we afford it?

"Oh my god," she shrieked, and held up the home pregnancy test, showing Robert. "We're pregnant again!"

Charlie turned to me and shrugged, a sheepish grin on his face. I bolted up and immediately felt faint. I wanted to run. Run away and never come back. I looked around like a trapped rabbit looking for a way to escape but before I could head for the door, Catherine was wrapping her arms around me.

"This is wonderful news. The best Christmas gift, ever. I'm so happy for you."

I forced a smile on my face. "I need to use the bathroom."

"Yes, yes. Of course. Charlie. Help your wife to the bathroom."

And there it was. I'd gone from being a person to the Bouchard's sacred vessel, someone in need of assistance to walk down the hall to the bathroom. Charlie was at my side and took my arm, guiding me out of the parlor while Catherine ordered Mac to bring in a new bottle of champagne and bubbly apple cider for me.

Stepping into the hallway, I saw red … both literally and figuratively. I wrenched my arm out of Charlie's grip, before turning to face him. "How could you? We agreed to wait until after the next appointment," I hissed.

"It's Christmas. What better time to announce? Besides,

what difference do a few days make? Now we can celebrate."

"I want to go home."

Charlie's eyes hardened. "Go to the bathroom then come back into the parlor. I'm having champagne and toasting our new baby with my parents. You can drive us home when I'm done." Then he turned and walked away.

Stunned, I started to cry silent tears as I rushed to the bathroom. In going against my wishes to wait to tell his mother, Charlie had picked his mother over me. Suddenly I saw my future and I knew that he would always choose her. My temples pounded as tears rolled down my cheeks. I was hurt, angry, and something else ... nauseous. I barely made it to the toilet in time.

And so, it began.

Chapter Thirteen

Paw Leg – Attention

Taking my daypack off the hook by the door is Rae's cue that I'm leaving. I wish I could tell her that I'll only be gone for an hour. That I'll be right back. All she knows is I'm leaving and she's not going with me. She whimpers and cries, imploring me with her sad brown eyes. She reaches up and places a paw on my thigh. I feel bad, as always, but with temperatures in the 90s, I can't leave her in the car even for a quick run into the grocery store.

Taking a knee, I wrap my arms around her body and whisper in her good ear, "I love you. I'll be right back." Then I give her a rigorous bottom rub before standing and walking out the door.

The click sound means she's gone. When the door doesn't

click, she comes back inside. But the door clicked. I hear the car's metal door open and shut with a clang. The rumble of the car is loud, then fades away. She is gone. I sit by the door listening. Waiting. Nope. She's gone. I wander around the house. My nose leads me to a piece of popcorn under a chair. I check my bowl. Nothing. I sniff around the bowl's edges and find a piece of kibble wedged between the wall and the bowl. I drink from my water bowl. Not too much. I don't know when my girl will be back.

The cold white box filled with good smells hums. I walk into the room where we sit on the couch. The big black box that sometimes is filled with moving pictures makes a high-pitch whine. I sniff. It is warm but not alive. I walk under the large table where my girl eats. I find a cracker. Above me, on the table, something is making a whirring noise. It also buzzes softly. I walk to the sleeping place where it is quiet. Onto the soft place where my girl sleeps, I curl into a ball and wait. I close my eyes.

There's a rumble from a car. I run to the door. The rumble stops. No door opens. My girl doesn't come. I run and jump on the couch. I stand so I can look through the screen. Across the street, sits a dark car. This is new. My nose works the air coming through the screen. Grass, pine trees, a trash can with rotting meat, and hot metal. Movement catches my eye. The car door opens, and a man climbs out. I work hard to catch his scent. The man closes the door. He turns and stares at me. Not moving. Standing and staring. Woof. He doesn't move. I bark again. Louder now. Woof, woof, woof. I hear a car coming. Moments later, the man turns in the

direction of the car sound. He looks down the street. He looks at
me again before walking up the steps to his house. I hear the tinkle
of keys. He opens the door and is gone. Woof, woof, woof. I scared
him away. Even though the room is filled with high-pitch whines
and buzzing sounds I stay on the couch. I lay down facing the door,
my head propped on the raised edge. I do not close my eyes. I wait.

Luca will be here soon along with Champ. We are going on what he calls a "sniff about" adventure for the dogs … whatever that is. Then for us, dinner, and a movie, here at my house. This is the first time he's been over—the first time anyone other than Frank has been to my house—and I'm as nervous as a baby bird about to leave the nest. It's a different kind of nervousness … not like I get when I worry about Charlie showing up someday. It's a good nervousness. An excited nervous.

After week three of Jiu-Jitsu, my jitters have begun to fade. I've stopped having nightmares about Charlie, which is a relief. I'm not sure if it's because I feel more confident—rightly or wrongly—or because I have something, or should I say someone else, on my mind. Not counting the hike with the dogs, this will be our third official date.

Between the classes and our dates, I'm learning more about Luca. He laughs easily with a warm chuckle, especially at the antics of our dogs. He's very patient, which is important since he has to wait for me to type to have a conversation. He is learning some basic sign language. He's even taught me a few new signs.

I'm relaxed around Luca. Except I'm not relaxed right now. I look around to make sure I haven't missed anything. I've dusted, vacuumed, and cleared the dining room table, stacking everything on my bed.

We will NOT be going in there. I hid the mess by closing the bedroom door. I'm still determined to take things slowly, although the urge to kiss him is almost overwhelming. I hope he feels the same.

Talking to Mom yesterday, I learned she hasn't seen Charlie in weeks. She's convinced that he's given up. I'm not, but I'm also not obsessing about it. I've gone out to dinner with Abby, in town, and went shopping in the village for a new dress—a little white sun dress with black shoulder straps and piping—which I'm wearing tonight for what Luca calls a "sniff about," whatever that is. I've dabbed a light perfume behind my ears in case more than the dogs want to sniff about. I smirk at my silliness.

Rae pops her head up. She cocks her head, listening intently. Seconds later, I hear a car approaching. Rae lets out a woof and runs to the door. I look out the front window. Luca's Jeep is pulling into the driveway next to my car, Champ's head sticking out the window. Champ barks. Hearing Champ's bark Rae barks again as she spins in circles at the front door.

By the time I open the door, Rae is beyond excited. She rushes to the passenger side of the car to bark at Champ. Luca opens the door for Champ, who leaps out, saunters over to the first bush he finds, and lifts his leg. Rae dances circles around him.

"Hey," Luca says all casual, while my heart flutters like the wings of a hummingbird.

Smiling, I raise my hand in reply.

"Look at you. I've never seen you in a dress before. I like it."

The compliment makes me glow with pleasure. I spin so the dress flares out in a circle around me. Pleased that he noticed, I make the sign for "thank you."

"Ready for a sniff about?"

"What?" I mouth, not sure what he means by "sniff about."

Luca understands and explains. "You'll need her leash and your phone. We are going on a very slow walk. There will be plenty of time to have a conversation while the dogs ferret out interesting smells. I wouldn't be surprised if it takes us an hour to simply walk around the block."

Oh … a sniff about. I get it. I head to the house and when I return, I hand my keys to Luca and clip the leash on Rae. Phone in hand, I'm ready. With Champ also on a leash now, we make it as far as the rose bush in my next-door neighbor's yard.

"First stop. Abby tells me you write newsletters. Anything I would have read?" Luca asks, as he pulls out his phone so he can read my texts.

With the end of Rae's leash wrapped around my wrist, my fingers type a text message telling him about my newsletters.

"That's interesting. Maybe the Academy needs a newsletter."

Maybe, although I don't comment. While I could use the money, I can't picture working for Luca. I'd rather crawl in bed with him.

"Here we go." Champ pulls Luca a full two feet away to another rose bush. Rae joins him and together they work at decoding who has been here before them.

"Someone compared what our dogs are doing to people using Facebook to find out about their friends. Dogs can find out who was here—boy or girl—what they had for dinner. Whether they are sick or healthy. Their sense of smell is 100,000 times more sensitive than ours. 100,000 times. Really incredible. Then I saw this documentary on dog senses and learned that a dog's nose has a thermal sensing component as well. They can detect warmth. I thought that was so interesting. The scientists think it's so newborn puppies can find their mother's teats before their eyes are open."

Wow, I mouthed. When Luca starts talking about his dog, or any dog, he gets a bit carried away. Champ is his best friend like Rae is mine, but sometimes I wish he'd look at me like I were his best friend. Baby steps, I tell myself as Luca continues.

"And then there is their vision. While they don't recognize bright colors—only blues and yellows—they have better night vision and can spot the tiniest of movements. And their hearing ... they can hear things as far away as a quarter mile. Their hearing is four times more sensitive than ours, plus they can hear sounds that we can't hear like your dog whistle. I just think it's fascinating," he

NO WORDS BETWEEN US

says, watching the two dogs work their noses from leaf to leaf.

I type, "You sure know a lot about dogs."

"I'm kind of a science nerd, so I end up watching a ton of science documentaries. What do you like to watch?"

Typing … "I'm partial to movies that are based on a true story. They are entertaining but you learn something at the same time. At the end of the movie, I Google how much of the movie was based on facts and how much was made up. I like books like that as well. Historical fiction. Do you read?"

The dogs pull us forward to a massive Jeffrey pine that must be a favorite pee stop. Rae has found an interesting scent and follows it around the tree, circling back to where the smell must be the strongest.

I know this dog. He marks here and on the fence post by my place. He is old. He eats bad food that makes him sick. He doesn't drink enough water. He is that big dog who only woofs once. One big loud bark. Not like the small dog who yaps, yaps, yaps when she walks by my house and sees me. The dog who lives behind the fence barks once then pauses, then barks, barks, barks.

Champ pulls to the other side of the tree. I pull my girl around the other way until Champ and I have our noses next to each other. I hear my girl and Champ's man laugh. A squirrel was here. I follow the scent up the tree as far as I can. I stand on my back legs to keep following the trail. Champ does the same. We both bark. Woof, woof, woof. The squirrel must be gone. Nothing chatters from above. No fun here.

We pull the dogs away from the tree and continue our sniff about. We are a full two houses away.

"At this rate, we won't even make it to the end of the block," I type.

"It doesn't matter. They are having fun. And so am I."

I look up at him and smile. Then I point to his phone. He didn't answer my question about what he likes to read.

"I read or should I say, listen. I use Audible, except for cookbooks. Listening allows me to work in the yard or clean the house while listening at the same time. It makes the tasks I hate more bearable. I also listen anytime I have to drive down the hill."

Hmm. What I heard was he doesn't like gardening, but he does do housework, although he doesn't like it, but then again, who does? "You don't like to garden? I love it," I type.

"If you saw my yard, you'd understand why. It's nothing but weeds. Every time it rains, the weeds come back. It's never-ending. I might enjoy growing food, since I love to cook, but it's so much work."

Fair enough. Growing your own food is a lot of work but the tomatoes taste like tomatoes and the apples are so much sweeter. The dogs pull us to another sweet spot, and we are paused again.

"Speaking of food, what are we having tonight?" he asks.

"A pizza with fresh veggies from the Community Garden. I love eating what I've grown. I've also made a salad with lettuce I picked today. Too early for tomatoes, though. Sorry. Then popcorn with the movie, of course."

Luca reads what I've written. "You're making me hungry. Let's cross the street and walk back. I have a bottle of red wine in the car."

I nod my agreement and then to my surprise, he takes my hand, and we cross the street together, the dogs leading the way. Looking down quickly at our hands, the tips of my little fingers peek out of his massive hand. I feel small but I also feel protected. It's not a bad feeling.

The pace back is quicker, like horses returning to the stables. When we come to the house across the street, Rae pulls to the left so she can sniff the tires of a black jeep parked in the driveway. Her nose is working overtime.

Luca looks at Rae. "The driver probably ran over something. Champ does the same thing."

I need two hands to pull Rae away so we can cross the street. Luca hands me my keys before retrieving a bottle of wine from his vehicle. While I unlock the front door, Rae stands on the porch, turning to stare at the house across the street. The place is one of those vacation rentals with occupancy and car limits posted on a placard to the left of the garage. Most of the time, the people who rent the place are well-behaved. But sometimes, a rowdy bunch makes a racket, and a neighbor calls the police. I lay low and keep out of it. Rae is alert, and watchful. The Jeep looks brand new and has temporary plates. There is nothing unusual about the house or the Jeep, but Rae is telling me otherwise.

Over a leisurely dinner we "talked" about our childhoods—me growing up in a commune, Luca growing up around his parent's Jiu-Jitsu studio. Then we move to the couch to watch one of my favorite dog movies, *Turner and Hooch*. When Tom Hanks tells Hooch, "No begging, no food, no sniffing of crotches, and you will not drink from my toilet!" Luca laughs for a full minute. Rae is begging for popcorn on my right and Champ is begging for popcorn on Luca's left. I place one popcorn kernel in my mouth and hand one to Rae. Luca is doing the same.

I watch her hand. Into the bowl, into her mouth. Into the bowl, one for me. Her, me, her, me. Wait. She forgot me. I put my paw on her leg. Hand in the bowl, one for me. Then she makes the sign for no more and shows me the empty bowl. Champ's man still has popcorn. I walk around and sit next to Champ. His hand goes into the bowl. One for the man, one for Champ, one for me. Now his bowl is empty. Champ curls up next to the man's feet. I walk around the low table. I jump on the couch. I curl into a ball next to my girl and place my head on her lap. She scratches my head. I let out a contented sigh. The big black box is filled with lights. I hear a dog bark and bark. I lift my head to listen. I don't know where this dog is. It's not Champ. The dog barks again. I jump down. I listen. I smell. More barking. I bark back. The man laughs. My girl makes a funny sound like birds chirping. I can't find the other dog in the room.

With only one good ear, Rae can't pinpoint the location of

the dog barks coming from the speaker under the television. I pat the couch for her to come back. She sniffs around and then returns.

Popcorn finished, Luca moves closer and drapes his arm across the back of the couch, his hand resting on my arm. I lean into him. My heart is beating like a small bird as I nestle under his protective wing. A sigh of contentment escapes my lips. He looks down at me and smiles. I want to say something without the damn tablet, without signs. I make a decision. Turning to face him, I tap him on his chest to pull his attention away from the television.

"Yeah?"

I motion with my hand for him to bring his face closer. I stretch up until my mouth is next to his ear. "I can whisper," I say in my barely-there voice.

He pulls away, a smile on his face. "So, you can. That's great." He reaches for the remote and hits mute before saying, "Tell me more." He leans down, offering me his ear.

"This is as loud as I can speak. The only way anyone can hear me is to move in real close. Up until now, there hasn't been anyone I've felt comfortable talking to in this way."

Without moving away, Luca says in a whisper of his own, "I can understand why. This feels very … intimate."

"Yes, it does," I whisper, a tingle of excitement spreading through my body.

Then he turns his face to mine, and we kiss. It starts slow, soft, and warm. Lips part and tongues explore patiently, testing, retreating, teasing, then moving deeper. At some point, Rae jumps off the couch allowing me to drape my leg over Luca's. When we finally come up for air, the movie is over and Rae and Champ are asleep, curled up next to each other.

"That was the sexiest dog movie ever. Who knew?" said Luca.

Shaking my head, I roll my eyes before leaning in, whispering, "That's why I picked it."

"I like that I can hear you. I'm glad you don't talk with everyone this way," he teases.

"You and my dog are the only ones."

"I'm honored."

"Of course, we can't do this in public. I'll be back to using signs and phones, but here we can talk."

Luca nods. "I agree. It wouldn't be professional to have you whispering to me in class, not to mention how you'd end up turning me on again. We can't have that, either. Extremely unprofessional."

Again. Yes. I'd felt his arousal and chose to ignore it, telling myself to slow down. We'd only been on three dates and besides, my bed is covered with files and computers. I want to stretch this out and enjoy the anticipation. I hope he feels the same.

"Let's have another conversation, next time at my place. I want to cook for you."

A man who cooks … music to my ears. Even though I can whisper, it's difficult. I keep my sentences short and to the point. I whisper, "I'd like that. When?"

"How about the Fourth of July? The academy is closed for the holiday, and we can spend the day together, including the dogs, of course. Maybe go to the parade then head back to my place to escape the tourist mobs. We can watch the fireworks from my deck."

Except for the sweet nothings I whisper to Rae every morning and night, I haven't talked this much in years and I'm paying for it now. My throat feels scratchy and rough. I give him a thumbs up and then tap my throat to indicate that I need something to drink.

Luca follows me into the kitchen. After I've downed a full glass of water, he wraps his arms around my waist.

"This was a good beginning. I like you, Lizzy Mueller. I like you a lot. I'm looking forward to spending more time together and continuing our conversation."

The way he says "conversation" sounds sexy and suggestive. I want to drag him and his hard-on into the bedroom, rip off his clothes and push him down onto my files and notebooks. Instead, I smile and mouth, "Me, too."

Rae and Champ join us in the kitchen, Rae drinking noisily from her bowl and Champ whining that he is ready to go home.

"It's past his bedtime," Luca laughs. Then to Champ, "Okay, okay. We're going."

Outside standing by Luca's Jeep, Luca pulls me into his arms for one last, long, sensual kiss that has me second-guessing my decision to send him home. The spell is broken by Rae barking.

Standing on the front porch, staring across the street, she's barking like she does at a squirrel except the squirrels are bedded down for the night high in the trees.

Looking across the street, nothing unusual catches my attention. The house is dark. The Jeep is still in the driveway. Shush, I say with my finger to my lips, but she keeps barking. I shake my head in an apology to Luca, then mouth the word, "Sorry." Pushing up on my tippy toes, I plant a kiss on his cheek before walking away.

"I'll text you tomorrow," he calls out before climbing behind the wheel and starting the engine.

I wave and continue to the porch where Rae is still barking. I want to ask her, What? What is it? She is bothered about something. I'm worried about the neighbors. I manage to pull Rae inside and close the door. Rae has stopped barking but now she is making that low growling sound that resonates deep in her chest, usually reserved for trespassing critters.

He was at the window. Watching. I don't like him. My girl doesn't understand. There is danger in that house. My girl heads into the room with the food and I follow. She opens the treat door. She snaps her fingers. I sit. She hands me a minty chew stick. I snatch it from her fingers and race for the couch. I have not forgotten the man across the street. I do not forget. But my girl is inside and safe. I have a chew stick. I am happy now.

Whatever it was that was making Rae crazy has been forgotten. I clean up the kitchen and head to bed, ready to collapse in a heap. When I open the bedroom door I am confronted by a mess. It takes me fifteen minutes to move files, notebooks, and computers back to the dining room table, change into a cool nightshirt, brush my teeth, and crawl under the covers. On cue, Rae leaps onto the bed, now with minty fresh breath, and curls up against my belly for our nighttime ritual. Happy thoughts of Luca swirl in my mind lulling me to sleep.

My girl falls asleep quickly tonight. No tossing and turning. I leave her and move to the couch. The room is warm. Air is whistling as it comes through the metal mesh covering the open window. On the couch, I make three turns in a circle before I curl into a ball. My eyes close. Then I hear it. My eyes pop open and my ears perk up. Loud banging sounds. Something is crashing. I turn my head. I stand with my front paws on the back of the couch and look out. The metal mesh makes the lights from other houses look pointy and sharp. The house across the street is dark. I hear a shout and another crash. I turn my head. My good ear faces the street. The noise is coming from that house. I growl, baring my teeth. I watch. Nothing moves. The noises stop. I wait. I watch.

Chapter Fourteen

Three Years Ago – March

Twenty-two weeks along with minimal nausea and a burst of new energy had me nesting like a mama stork. At my twelve-week appointment, Charlie and I heard the baby's heartbeat. The nurse worked the wand over my swollen abdomen and proclaimed, "There!" pointing at what looked like a third leg.

"Is that what I think it is?" Charlie asked.

The nurse nodded. "It's a boy. Do you want a picture?"

"You bet I do," Charlie said. "Wait 'til Mom sees this. Will his little penis show up in the photo?"

"Geez, Charlie!"

The nurse laughed. "Yes unless the little fellow shifts his position or crosses his legs before I can get the picture."

Charlie's smile was so wide I thought his face was going to crack open like an egg.

"Lizzy don't move."

"Don't tell me. Tell our son," I giggled.

Happiness swelled inside of me, so much so that I hadn't even minded when Charlie rushed out of the room to call his mother. His excited voice reverberated down the hall and I heard a nurse ask him to talk quieter or "take it outside." After I dressed, I joined Charlie, who was sitting in his car, still talking excitedly to his mother.

"She wants to talk to you," he said, handing me the phone.

"A boy! Marvelous news, just marvelous. I'm so very glad you decided to stop working. I think it's made a big difference, don't you?"

She didn't wait for me to answer before continuing. "I knew this one was a boy. I just knew it. You weren't sick like you were with that first one. I wasn't sick with my boys either."

That first one's name was Claire. I let it pass. Nothing could ruin my good mood, not even Catherine. Charlie and I spent the drive home bouncing baby names around. I liked Sam, he liked Liam, and we both knew Catherine would want the baby to be named Charles Robert after her son and husband. We knew this since she'd told us numerous times.

It had been a great day and we celebrated by stopping at Las Brisas for dinner. It was too cold to sit outside, so we requested a window seat with a view of the ocean, which we never glanced at once. Charlie ordered champagne and I had a bubbly lemon-lime soda in a champagne flute so I could pretend I was drinking champagne as well. We toasted little Sam Liam. Then a second toast for Liam Sam, and a third for Charles Robert. I found myself placing my hand protectively on my belly thinking, I will love you no matter what your name is, even if it's Charles Robert.

I'd been gardening out on my deck in raised beds for the past month. Charlie purchased two ADA elevated planters after Catherine had objected to the strenuousness of gardening. The beds were about two feet off the ground allowing me to sit while playing in the dirt. After Charlie filled the planters with soil, I planted arugula, which was growing like weeds, along with kale, spinach, and leeks in one of the two-by-eight-foot beds. Carrots and radishes were popping up in the other bed, where I'd saved room for a tomato plant once it warmed up a bit.

I'd thought I'd miss work but was surprised to discover I didn't. I slept in, read books (mostly about babies and parenting), gardened, and had time to cook gourmet meals that Charlie said were even better than the hospital meals he had loved so much. I'd purchased a book on how to make baby food and planned to make a batch once my carrots were mature. Charlie surfed, went to work, surfed, and came home directly after sunset. He'd make a fire, open a bottle of beer, and cuddle with me on the couch while I talked his ear off about my exciting day. Those were the good days.

The not-so-good days were when the waves were flat, and he had to spend an entire day at the office. Charlie had resigned from the family's foundation board to take a position with The Bouchard Company. With our growing family, his mother convinced him that he needed to "up his game," make more money and learn the family business. As the heir apparent, Charlie was being groomed to take over. A month of job shadowing his father had left Charlie grumpy and irritable, especially on days when the waves were calling.

Charlie confided in me—with a promise never to tell his parents, especially his mother—that he did have a dream job and it wasn't the family business. He wanted to start a surfing school for grommets or groms ... kids. I loved the idea and imagined our son learning to surf with his father while I waved from my balcony garden.

Today was one of those perfect California days at the beach ... no fog obscuring the blue sky, seagulls gliding past the balcony at eye level, and warm enough to only need a sweatshirt. Using my copper watering can, I was gently drizzling water around the bunches of spinach when my smart watch alerted me to an incoming call. A glance at the watch let me know it was Catherine. For a moment, I considered letting her call go to voicemail, but I knew that would be putting off the inevitable since she'd keep calling until I picked up. She had bought me the watch for this very reason so that she could reach me morning, noon, or night ... for my safety, of course.

"Hello," I said, as I headed indoors.

"How are you feeling?"

"I feel great. Eating well, gaining weight. All good," I said as I placed the watering can in the sink to be filled again.

"Wonderful. I am so glad to hear it." Then she paused, which sent off internal alarm bells. "I wanted to talk to you about Charlie."

This couldn't be good. I made myself comfortable in the corner of the couch with my feet propped on the coffee table. She didn't wait for me to encourage her to continue. Catherine never needed encouragement when she had something to say.

"Charlie is not taking his responsibilities with the company seriously. When the surf is good, he shows up late and leaves early. What kind of example is he setting for his employees? It's embarrassing, but don't tell him I said that."

Catherine kept asking me to keep things from Charlie, one of the many things she did that rubbed me the wrong way.

"Of course not," I assured her, not from any sense of loyalty to Catherine but because I knew it would piss Charlie off.

"I'm hoping you can talk to him. Make him understand how important this job is to you and your growing family. If he hears it from you, he'll listen."

The family business was not my husband's passion. I knew it and so did Catherine, but I agreed to talk to him. What I wanted to tell her was that this was her fault. She was the one who bought her boy a house overlooking a perfect point break. It was like leaving a line of cocaine on a mirror every morning for an addict. What did she expect?

"When do you think you'll broach the subject? Make sure he's in a good mood, though. And whatever you do, don't tell him I asked you to do this."

"Of course," I said again, tiring of the conversation. "Hey, Catherine. Little Sammy is pressing on my bladder." I patted my belly. Thanks, Buddy, for always providing the perfect exit strategy.

"Sure, sure. Sorry to keep you. Just one more thing ... can you have "the talk" before Friday? There is an important meeting with all the senior officers that Charlie needs to attend. He'll have to miss his morning surf."

We both knew that if the waves were over two feet, that was never going to happen, but I said I'd do my best and hung up. What Catherine didn't know and couldn't control was what I was going to say, because if she did, she wouldn't have asked me to talk to Charlie.

A week had passed since Catherine asked me to talk with Charlie. We talked, or more accurately, Charlie talked, and I listened as he launched into a rant. Charlie described the unbearable weight of his mother's expectations as being caught in a rip tide. If you swam directly into the rip, you would tire and drown. The way to free yourself from the tide's pull was to swim perpendicular to the current until you were free of its influence.

This morning, Charlie was ready to swim free. My head swiveled from left to right and back again as Charlie paced between the kitchen and the living room.

"I can't believe I'm going to cut the cord. You know she's going to use this house as leverage, pulling it out from under us. Maybe she won't because of the baby. I can use that. I can tell her if she decides to play dirty then say goodbye to her grandson because we'll be forced to move, north to Santa Cruz. There's amazing surfing in Santa Cruz, but it's a bit rough in the winter. Maybe not Santa Cruz."

Moving away wasn't part of the plan but it was good ammunition in the battle for Charlie's independence. He'd been in several of these skirmishes before and rarely won. But this time it would be different. I was in his corner.

Charlie rambled on, building his courage as he formulated his arguments.

"I've never wanted to be part of your mega empire, that was Phillip's dream, not mine. And now that he is gone, you can't make me into your favorite son. I don't care about the money—"

That was easy to say when you had a trust fund that would allow you to live comfortably, but I didn't interrupt. He was on a roll.

"—money doesn't make you happy. Look at you and dad."

"Maybe you shouldn't say that thing about her and Robert," I suggested from my corner of the couch. "It's going to piss her off more unless that's your intention."

Charlie shrugged. "She's going to be livid no matter what I say. I can hear her arguments in my head … I'm shirking my responsibilities. I'm afraid of success. It's my birthright. I owe it to Grandpa and Dad. I've heard it all before. It's the refrain from the song of my life. This time, though, I have a secret weapon."

I cocked my head. "What's that?"

"You. You have given me the courage to stand up for myself."

And stand up for me as well.

Charlie's phone beeped, alerting him that he needed to go. He fortified himself with his cold coffee, before pulling me to a standing position.

Wrapping his arms around me he whispered in my ear, "Babe, wish me luck. She can be a tsunami when things aren't going her way."

Giving him an extra squeeze, I said, "You can do this." I hoped I was right.

Grabbing my purse, I followed him to the garage door.

"Where are you going?" he asked, holding the door open for me.

"Twenty-two-week doctor's appointment."

"That's today? Damn. I wanted to be there for all of your appointments. Maybe I should cancel my meeting. I can move it to tomorrow or even next week."

"No, no, no. It took over a month to pin her down. You're ready. Go. I'll be fine. It's just a routine appointment."

Charlie nodded and forced a smile. "I much rather be going with you than face the dragon lady."

"If she starts breathing fire, imagine teaching little Sammy—"

"You mean Liam," he teased.

"—to surf along with the other kids in your school. That is your shield."

Charlie pecked me on the cheek then climbed into his car. He gave me a thumbs up through the windshield before he backed out of the garage. I imagined the celebration we'd have that evening and decided to stop for a bottle of champagne for Charlie on the way home from my appointment.

"Good morning, Mrs. Bouchard," the nurse said, looking at my chart.

"You can call me Lizzy." This nurse was new to me. I'd already trained the other nurses and my doctor to call me Lizzy. To me, Mrs. Bouchard was Charlie's mother.

"Twenty-two weeks … well into the second trimester. How are you feeling?"

"Pretty good. No nausea, I'm eating, and I have tons of energy. I've had this low, dull backache, but that must be from all the gardening. Otherwise, I feel great."

The nurse wrote down my responses and then placed the blood pressure cuff around my arm. Moments later… "Blood pressure looks good. Have you felt any movement yet?"

I shook my head.

"Don't worry. Most women feel movement between

sixteen and twenty-four weeks. You should feel something real soon. You're having a boy. Any names yet?"

"Either Sam or Liam," I said.

"Like Liam Hemsworth?"

"Maybe. It's my husband's choice. I'm not sure where he came up with the name."

"Go ahead and lay back."

I adjusted the pillow under my head and gathered my shirt under my breasts to expose my swollen belly, which was the size of a soccer ball. As she rolled the ultrasound station next to me and squeezed the cold gel onto the wand, she kept talking about Liam Hemsworth ... how she loved him in all the Thor movies and how handsome he is. The more she talked the more determined I was NOT to name my little boy Liam. She angled the cart to give me a better view of the monitor, moving the wand across my belly, as she chatted away.

"There he is," she said. "Now let's hear his heartbeat."

She applied gel to the same instrument the doctor had used when we first heard our baby's heartbeat, then pressed it into my abdomen, moving it up and down to find the perfect spot.

We waited. "I don't hear anything," I said, feeling a tingle of apprehension at the nape of my neck.

"Let me check the volume." She fiddled with a dial. "Sometimes these things act up. I'll be back with the doctor."

It's probably broken, I told myself, fighting off the dread that threatened to overwhelm me. The look of concern on my doctor's face when she entered the room did nothing to alleviate my fears.

"Something's wrong. Why can't we hear the heartbeat?" I asked, knowing the answer but praying I was wrong.

"Let me take a look," Dr. Trish said, picking up the wand and pressing it into my flesh.

For what seemed like an eternity, no one spoke … not the nurse, not the doctor, not me. I was straining to hear the tiniest blip—willing my baby to move, to live.

Dr. Trish handed the wand to the nurse.

"No," I whispered. "Please, no. It's there. I know it's there."

"I'm so sorry, Lizzy," she said, grasping my hand. "There is no heartbeat."

Chapter Fifteen

Thigh Slap – Come

I slept like the dead last night … no weird dreams, no nightmares, or Rae barking. She's been making this deep growling sound each night and then a sharp bark, which wakes me just as I'm drifting off. But not last night. Last night we both slept like hibernating bears.

Rae pops onto the bed around six and curls up in a ball pressed against my stomach, falling back asleep after tucking her paws in just so. I am fully awake, my arm draped over her body, my fingers weaved into her silky fur. I stare out the sliding glass door at the patches of robin-egg blue sky between the pine trees getting excited about the day ahead. We'll need to get up soon if we are going to snag a decent spot along the Fourth of July parade route. The only improvement to this moment would be if Luca was spooning my backside, making me the center of a cuddle cookie.

Sometimes, but not often, I let myself imagine what it would have been like if I'd had kids ... lazy mornings in bed, tiny feet kicking and squirming under the blankets, nose kisses, hair tousles. When I first moved to Pine City, my feelings were like a gaping open wound. Thoughts of children would launch me on a crying jag that would leave me as limp as a wilted flower. But Rae has changed all that. I find that I can think about children again without falling apart. I'm still sad about the two angels I lost, Claire and Sammy, but it doesn't destroy me like it used to.

Rae sits up and stretches by pointing her nose at the ceiling before turning to give me morning kisses—licking my throat with her long pink tongue up to my chin. My throat must be the cleanest part of my body since she does this every morning and night. I move before she licks my face completely off.

I let Rae outside before heading to the bathroom. Rae barks once and I let her back in. Bark in, bark out, repeat. The story of my life. Rae is walking with a limp, favoring her back leg. I check her out and find a small pinecone stuck to the long fur on her leg.

Pinecone removed, tea steeping, holiday-appropriate clothing on (a pair of denim Daisy Dukes, a short sleeve white blouse, with a red bandana around my neck), I drop a slice of bread into the toaster and pull out the butter. The phone rings and I assume it's Luca asking where we are going to meet, but instead it's Mom.

"Happy Fourth," she says, sounding extremely chipper for eight in the morning.

I type back, "Happy Fourth," as I butter my toast.

"Sorry to call so early, but Eric and I are heading to the beach to stake out a spot for the day. We're trying to snag one of the fire pits, but other people will have the same idea, so we might not get one. We're bringing umbrellas, two huge blankets, firewood, an ice chest, and enough food to last the entire day. Once we've marked our spot, we're going to ride bikes from the beach back into town for the parade. Isn't that a great idea? Eric is a real thinker. This way we'll avoid the parade traffic in the morning and then we'll already have our spot at the beach for the fireworks. They shoot them over the ocean. Oh, why am I telling you? You used to live at the beach. Anyway, Eric says we'll enjoy two shows … one in the sky and one in the water. Isn't that amazing?"

From what I've gathered so far, Eric, Mom's latest beau, could be a keeper. He has a job, and his own house, and apparently is a "real thinker."

I type, "Sounds like a fun day."

"Hey, how did you like the card I sent you? I thought it was hilarious. I'm surprised you didn't call me as soon as you opened it."

Now that I think about it, I realize I didn't receive a Fourth of July card. Normally, I would have noticed, but between Jiu-Jitsu, Luca, the garden, Rae, and my newsletter business, my mind has been fully occupied.

"Your card never came," I write and add a sad face.

"Oh no. It was so cute. You would have loved it. Let me see if I can remember what it said … there was a picture of Abe Lincoln on the front and it said, 'Time to Get Star Spangled' and then when you open the card there's a picture of a six-pack of beer and it says, 'Hammered.' Get it? Star Spangled Hammered. I thought it was a hoot. Now I'm bummed that the card didn't arrive. It's weird because I mailed it weeks ago with 'Do Not Open Until the 4th' written on the back. Are you sure the envelope isn't stuck between your bills or in a magazine or something?"

While Mom talks and talks, I load my backpack with water, Rae's collapsible bowl, a baggie of dog treats, and a granola bar.

"I haven't seen it. Sorry. Hey, I'm taking off for a parade as well and have to leave if I want to find a parking spot. Enjoy the day." I add a flag and fireworks emoji to my text.

It takes a good minute before Mom responds, still talking about the lost card and how the post office here in Pine City is probably to blame.

"A parade? Good for you. Parking is always an issue at these things. I'm glad you are leaving early. That's why we're riding our bikes. So clever, don't you think? Oh, wait. I forgot why I called. I sent you a package. It's supposed to arrive tomorrow around ten. I sent it using UPS since your post office is unreliable. Anyway, have a great day. Love you."

Wow. She must be in a good mood. She doesn't usually sign off with "I love you." This Eric guy could be the reason. If so, he's definitely a keeper. I'm about to tuck my phone in my back pocket when a ping alerts me to an incoming text.

"Where are we meeting?"

It's Luca. I have a feeling he is a keeper as well. "I'm thinking near the start of the parade route so we can make a quick getaway. Afterward, I need to stop by the community garden to water and pick some veggies for our salad tonight. Then we can leave. I don't plan on going back into town until all the tourists have left."

"Parking near Main and Oliver. Bringing two chairs. C U in 10."

Luca can be a man of few words when he's texting while I tend to write more than is necessary. But in my defense, I don't talk so writing is all I have. Then again, it could be hereditary. I respond with a thumbs-up emoji and leave it at that.

I watch Lizzy. She has treats in the bigger bag with the two straps. That means I'm going. When she takes the small bag, it means sometimes, not always, I must stay. I do not like to stay alone. Lizzy takes my long strap and hooks it to my collar. Another sign that I'm going. I bark for joy. I love walks. But instead of walking, we climb into the car. That's okay. As long as I'm with my girl, I'm happy. It's warm inside here. Lizzy makes the clear walls vanish so I can hang my head outside. My nose twitches, working to pull in smells from the moving air that makes my fur fly... cut grass, those sweet-smelling trees, stale water, and something else. I turn and look back. The black car. It's moving. It's following us. I bark. I do not like the black car that sits all day across the street. That car ran over an animal. A squirrel. I can smell it. The watcher who stands outside at night lives with the black car. The car is still following. I bark again.

I'm glad Rae is enjoying the ride. Her long ears fly away from her face like two ends of a woman's scarf in the wind. She's barking at something behind us. Probably a squirrel. She hates squirrels for some reason. When she barks a second time, I check my rearview mirror. The neighbor's black Jeep is trailing behind us. The people who are renting the house across the street are quiet and keep to themselves … the perfect renters. Rae barks again and I reach over and give her a good rub on her backside, which brings her back inside for more.

Ten minutes later, I find a parking spot two blocks away from Main and Oliver. The black Jeep rolls past, presumably looking for a spot as well. The dark tinted windows make it impossible to see inside.

Backpack on my shoulders, Rae pulling on the leash, we make our way through the gathering crowd of red, white, and blue festooned tourists and locals. I stop at the curb and look up and down the street for Luca. Rae spots him first and barks. He is standing and waving from across the street about a half block down from the intersection. We walk down the center of the street that has been closed off to traffic for the parade. Luca is still standing when we arrive at our spot. He wraps his arms around me in a bear hug as the two dogs sniff noses and then butts. I'm glad humans don't greet each other the same way.

Once I'm settled in the camp chair and Rae's bowl is filled with water, Luca hands me a cup of iced Chai tea, which I appreciate since it's already in the high 70s. It's supposed to be a scorcher in Southern California, even up here in the mountains. I pull out my phone so we can converse before the parade starts, the dogs lie at our feet.

After some back and forth covering the weather, the crowd, the tourists, and what he will be grilling tonight for dinner, Luca asks about the Jiu-Jitsu class.

"You're about halfway through the course. We are about to move into more aggressive attacks. Do you think you're ready?"

I nod and shrug at the same time. "Can we ever really be ready for a violent attack?" I type.

To his credit, Luca pauses and doesn't spout some flippant reply. "You're right. I've never been attacked. I'm hoping the class gives you tools to defend yourself and the confidence to use them. You won't know if you're ready until something happens … which I hope never does."

When he says this last part, he reaches over and takes my hand, squeezing it but not letting go. Since I can't type an answer, I nod and mouth, me too. Luca's holding my right hand, I'm holding my tea in my left, Rae is lying on my feet, and all is right in the world. We watch in silence, Luca occasionally bumping my shoulder with his and then cocking his head where he wants me to look. Once it was a pair of Dachshunds dressed like hot dogs and their owners dressed like ketchup and mustard. Another time, it was two little girls dressed as sparklers with sequined leotards and a spray of silver tinsel pinned to the tops of their heads.

People have red, white, and blue tattoos, red, white, and blue clothing, and even patriotic camp chairs. One guy has an American flag painted on his face. I turn and look at Luca. He is dressed in khaki shorts and a hibiscus pattern Hawaiian shirt in pinks and greens. I disengage my hand so I can ask him a question.

"Where is your red, white, and blue?" I type.

He leans in close and whispers one word, "Underwear." Then pulls away, giving me a mischievous smile that goes all the way to the corners of his eyes.

I shake my head, then type. "I don't believe you."

Luca doesn't seem like the kind of person who owns patriotic underwear.

He laughs and says, "I'll prove it to you later."

Before I can make a sarcastic reply, the first marching band comes strutting down the street. Horns are blaring, drums beating, and the drum major looks like he is in danger of throwing his shoulder out with his enthusiastic thrusts of his silver baton.

What is this? It's so loud. Why are people walking that way? They don't look right. I turn and look at my girl. She isn't worried. She's smiling. I look at Champ's man. He is smiling, too. Champ hasn't moved from his place at the man's feet. He doesn't lift his head. I lie down again only to pop back up. Strange people with large, round noses, giant feet, big hair, and strange clothes are throwing bits of sugar at the crowd. One lands at my feet. I sniff. It's sweet but wrapped in something that I cannot eat. Small people run into the street and take the bits of sugar. The large-footed strangers clomp past. My girl picks up a sweet and shows it to her man.

My nose goes wild. Coming down the street are giant four-legged animals with people sitting on top of them. Even Champ lifts his head and then his nose. They are animals, but I am confused by the sound their feet make when they hit the ground. It sounds different. Champ looks at the animals, snorts, then drops his head. The metal-footed animals move on. Then a high-pitched whine catches my attention. Strange people are riding small, two-wheeled machines that race and whine. The people are holding on tight as the machines speed in circles. The people are wearing large caps that swallow their heads. I do not like this. One of these machines comes close to my girl. I bark and then hide behind her chair.

Rae is freaked out by the Shriners on their minibikes. Poor thing. This must be so confusing for her. For the first twelve months of her life, Rae has had limited contact with the outside world. This is the first time she's been exposed to the kaleidoscope of humanity in all its outrageousness. I slap my thigh for her to come. I pull on her leash and slap my thigh again. Two more slaps and Rae jumps onto my lap where I bend to whisper into her good ear, "It's okay. It's okay."

Another marching band, followed by the high school cheer

squad, then more horses, which has Rae climbing off my lap to move closer to the animals. Her little black nose is working overtime as one of the horses drops a load a few feet away from us. I hear a little boy yell, "Gross!" which makes the adults around us laugh in agreement. The green road apples are deftly scooped up with a giant shovel by a rodeo clown inside a barrel, pulling a trash can on wheels behind him.

There is an assortment of antique cars slowly passing in front of us, the passengers tossing candy out the windows for the kids. I hear Rae growling but not like her low humming of concern she reserves for something moving in the yard. This is a genuine growl … deep and menacing. I turn around. A woman is walking behind us with a small brown dog on a leash. The little dog is straining at the end of his leash but not barking. Odd. Rae doesn't usually growl at other dogs.

Then I look beyond the woman to a man standing directly behind us watching the parade. His head is covered by a huge Uncle Sam head. He's wearing a red, white, and blue suit. Rae looks like she wants to kill him. More growling before she erupts into staccato barking like I've never heard before.

"What's wrong?" Luca asks, as people begin to look at Rae like she's rabid.

Using both hands, I pull Rae back in front of me. People in masks freak her out. She is right about one thing … that guy looked creepy. Turning around, I give the sign for "sorry" before holding Rae close to me, her growls rumbling deep in her chest.

"It's okay," I whisper until finally, Rae stops. Looking behind me again, the man in the mask is gone.

Back at the house, I'm washing lettuce, spinach, tomatoes, and carrots I harvested from my garden plot as Rae sits at my feet hoping for a treat. I give her a carrot. She sniffs the orange vegetable as if I'm trying to poison her and decides it's not for her. She walks over to the cupboard where I keep her dental chews, sits, and barks.

Treat. I want a treat. Bark. I don't know what that other thing was. It didn't smell like a treat. My girl looks at me but doesn't open the cupboard. I look at the cupboard. I look at her. Bark. Why doesn't she get me a treat? Doesn't she understand? I walk over and put my paw on her leg. She pushes my paw away. Sigh. I leave the kitchen. Nothing for me here. I head to the sleeping room, jump on the bed, and curl up. Lizzy comes in. She takes a huge bag from the small room with all her clothes. This is new. I sit up. She puts her sleeping clothes in the bag. She adds the stick that she puts in her mouth which makes her breath smell like candy. She places more clothing in the bag. What does this mean? I whine. I am anxious. My girl rubs my head. She touches my nose with hers.

Rae knows something's up. I don't know how, but she knows. From the moment I moved to Pine City, I've never packed an overnight bag because I've never spent a single night anywhere else but here, and neither has Rae. A big adventure awaits us.

Loading the car, Rae rushes past me and jumps inside. She does not want to be left behind. The salad is on the backseat nestled between my overnight bag and my backpack. On the drive to Luca's house, Rae has her head out the window, her nose working overtime. I come to a stop at a signal next to a truck with a Husky sitting in the backseat, his head is out the window, too. Rae says hello with a single bark. The Husky ignores her. Rae tries again to no avail before the light changes, and we drive on. Rae tires of the view and curls up in a ball on the seat, but as soon as I turn down the street to the Jiu-Jitsu academy Rae pops up. She knows where we are.

When I open her door, she rushes to the entrance of the academy, but that's not where we're going today. Standing at the corner of the building, I slap my thigh three times and Rae comes. We walk along the side of the building to the back where there are stairs leading up to a second-story deck where Champ barks a hello. Luca's home is on the second floor of the back half of the academy. The deck looks over a meadow filled with summer grasses and then beyond to the forested mountains. From here we will have an unobstructed view of the sky over the lake where the fireworks will explode.

"Welcome. Here let me get that," Luca says, meeting me halfway down the stairs.

With my bag and backpack on a lounge chair and the salad on the picnic table, my hands are free for a more intimate welcome. The kiss is long and deep, holding promise for what lies ahead. I feel tingles from my lips to my toes but what amazes me more is the opening of my heart. The heaviness that I've been carrying since the miscarriage and my traumatic brush with death feels lighter when I'm with Luca. I feel at peace, calm and safe.

Luca leans away to point out his view, but I pull him back for a second kiss. The first kiss was delicious. Why not have another?

Luca shows me what he thinks of my salad by having three helpings. We—Rae, Champ, Luca, and me—all think the chicken is delish, evidenced by the fact that there isn't a morsel left. While I enjoyed our light banter over dinner, my favorite part of the evening is now. We are cuddled together on an outdoor couch, dogs at our feet, a blanket over our legs, as we watch the fireworks. I make tiny ohhh and ahhh sounds at the bursts of colors painting the black sky. I imagine my mom watching the fireworks over the ocean and wonder if maybe next year we will watch from the edge of the lake. That's when I realize that I'm starting to think of Luca as a long-term boyfriend.

I stretch and whisper in his ear, "Next year, we should watch the fireworks by the lake. There'll be fireworks in the sky and their reflections on the water."

Luca turns to look at me. "I'd like that."

Interpreting his reply to mean that he, too, believes we'll be together next year as well, I give his thigh an affectionate squeeze.

An hour later, the fireworks are over, and all traces of our meal have been cleared away. We walk the dogs in the meadow so they can do their duty before climbing up the stairs. We stand at the deck railing and watch the headlights of the line of cars making their way off the mountain along the north shore.

"Ready?" Luca asks.

I nod before Luca leads me inside, the dogs at our heels.

Oh, what a night! My body is still glowing as I unpack my bag. I lift my nightshirt to my nose in hopes of finding a lingering scent of my man. Our lovemaking started slow and tender before shifting into hot and passionate, leaving us satiated and spent by the time we fell asleep. My wish to be in the middle of a cuddle cookie was granted when Rae joined Luca and me, curling up at my stomach as Luca pressed against my back. Then this morning, we enjoyed a more leisurely exploration in the soft filtered light coming through the white muslin drapes, which made me feel as though we were making love in the clouds.

I'm drying off after taking a hot, steamy shower when I hear Rae barking at the door. That's when I remember the package Mom said was going to be delivered today. Bathrobe on, towel still on my head, I rush to the door. Rae is barking wildly and growling. She doesn't like the mailman, or people in masks, and now I can add the UPS driver to her list of persons non-grata. I stomp and clap, but she isn't stopping. I open the door, ready to sign for the package, and there he is, Charlie.

"Hello, Babe. Did you miss me?"

Chapter Sixteen

Three Years Ago – April

Almost making it to the third trimester, I'd thought I was in the clear ... smooth sailing right up to delivery but I was wrong, so very wrong. I woke up sobbing, my pillow wet. Apparently, I had been crying in my sleep. No wonder Charlie hadn't been sleeping with me these past weeks. My grief was often loud, extroverted, and messy, while Charlie's was silent, hidden, and neat.

He tried to cheer me up by saying things like, "We'll try again. We're going to have lots of kids. You'll see."

This was the last thing I wanted to hear after going through labor to deliver our dead son. My doctor had advised me that if I wanted to become pregnant again, it would be better to be induced instead of having a D&C. Charlie was also in favor of a natural delivery. It had been easy for him to agree with the doctor since he wouldn't be having contractions for twenty-four hours straight.

I was induced, but not with an IV drip since it was too early in my pregnancy for my body to react to Pitocin. Instead, a pill was inserted into my cervix, every four hours until I was dilated enough to deliver. While this was painful, what hurt more was hearing the cries of other babies on what would forever be known as their birthday. Knowing that my baby would never cry, never celebrate a birthday, and never take his first breath, made every contraction so much more painful. My baby would be born silent. He would have no voice.

At first, I couldn't imagine looking at him. I thought it would drive the final stake into my already broken heart. But when the nurse told me he looked like a perfect baby that would fit in the palm of my hand, I knew I would regret it forever if I didn't hold him.

The color of his skin—a dark lavender, his lips a deep purple—took me by surprise, but he had ten fingers, ten toes, and a nose the size of a pea. He weighed next to nothing, almost four ounces I was told later, and I felt he was light enough to fly away.

After I'd been home for about a week, I had the most comforting dream. A bright purple bird with a deep purple beak sat on the limb of a winter tree, bare of leaves. The bird's face morphed into that of a beautiful child, still purple, but smiling. The bird/child took flight, gliding down from the branch, coming closer and closer until I could hear his voice.

"Thank you," he whispered as quietly as a leaf falling, before turning, and with a mad flapping of wings, shot into the air heading directly into the blinding light of the sun.

Well, I didn't need a psychologist to explain what *that* dream was all about. The dream touched me in a way all the condolence cards and flowers never did. I spent an hour online looking at images of purple birds, finally picking a violet-backed starling as the bird that would represent my lost little boy.

I felt bad that I hadn't had a similar dream for Claire. Then it hit me. I don't need a dream to tell me how to remember my daughter. Twenty minutes later, I'd decided the bluish-green Bee Hummingbird—the smallest of all birds at a mere two and a quarter inches long, even smaller than my baby girl—would represent Claire.

I printed images of the starling and the hummingbird and taped them on the closet door where the setting sun would light them like actors on a stage. Later, I spent two hundred and fifty dollars on a painting of a violet-backed starling in flight from a wildlife artist I found online. Then another three hundred on an oil painting of a Bee Hummingbird sitting on a branch from the same artist.

Charlie's reaction … "What's with all the birds?"

Since he'd abandoned me after only six hours of labor and wasn't there when Sammy was born, I felt he had lost his right to know. He never asked about Sammy … what he looked like, how big he was, nothing. So, nothing is what I told him. Not about the baby's coloring, his perfect little fingers, and toes, the dream, or the birds. The birds were mine and mine alone.

For the first three weeks, I had to wear pads for the bleeding, and a sports bra (one size too small) to compress my breasts to stop my milk from coming in. In week four, I finally moved out of the bedroom to the living room where I made a nest in the corner of the couch … blankets, pillows, a cup of tea, a book, a magazine, and my phone, all within arm's reach. While I was mourning, Charlie was surfing … first thing in the morning and two hours before sunset. We all handle grief differently. He surfs. I cry.

Week five after the miscarriage, Catherine called. There was an important meeting and Charlie was nowhere to be found. He wasn't answering his phone or responding to her text messages or emails. Because of my distraught call from the doctor's office, Charlie never had that well-rehearsed conversation with his mother about leaving the family business to start his surfing school. With the loss of the baby, Charlie has lost what little courage he had to confront his mother.

In a voice that sounded dead, even to me, I answered, "He's surfing."

While Catherine was the head cheerleader of team Pregnant Lizzy, she was missing in action when it came to miscarriages and stillbirths. A living, healthy, grandson was all that interested her. I had lost all patience with my mother-in-law and my two-word answers were all I was willing to give her.

"When he comes home, please tell him to call me. His

position with the company is in jeopardy and frankly, so is that beautiful house he loves so much."

"Sure." I hit "End" before she could say another hurtful word.

Charlie came home well after the sun had disappeared over the horizon. I'd been too apathetic to turn on lights as I watched the sky change from yellow to orange, from red to purple, and finally to black, a color that matched my mood. I was curled up in my nest, enjoying the darkness when I heard Charlie come through the door.

"Hey, why is it so dark in here?" he asked as he lit his progress from the garage door to the kitchen by flipping on every light switch along the way.

When he turned on both the kitchen light and the lights over the couch, I had to shield my eyes from the glare.

"Please turn these lights off," I asked, pointing up at the canned ceiling lights.

"Sure, but I'm leaving the kitchen light on. I need to be able to see where I'm going."

I heard him open the refrigerator. "Are we out of beer?"

"Unless you picked some up on the way home, yes."

"Geez, Lizzy. I thought you were going to go shopping today."

He walked over and stood in front of me. I pulled my blanket up to my chin defensively.

"How long are you going to do this? It's been almost a month. It's time to rejoin the living."

"Grief takes its own sweet time." I'd read that online.

"You need to get back on the horse and for god's sake, take a shower. You're starting to smell," he said, picking up the controller and turning on the TV.

He was right. I hadn't showered in four days. Tossing the blanket aside, I stood. At the bottom of the stairs, I fired off a salvo of my own.

"Your mother called. She wants you to call her back. She says she's going to take the house away from us if you don't start showing up for work."

"That fucking bitch," trailed after me as I climbed the stairs. Something crashed. I didn't care. A shower was sounding like the perfect place to hide.

By the time I came back downstairs in a clean pair of flannel pants, a white t-shirt, and my bathrobe, I felt hungry for the first time all day. I ran my fingers through my damp hair as I stood in front of the open refrigerator.

I really should have gone to the grocery store today, I thought, as I closed the fridge and opened a cupboard. I found a bag of egg noodles and I knew we had butter. Butter on noodles … a feast fit for a queen.

Normally, Charlie would have asked what I was making for dinner, but he was strangely quiet. He sat staring at his reflections in the sliding glass door, the television off. His disembodied voice floated across the space between us and sent a shiver down my spine.

"We need to have another baby."

I shook my head. He wasn't looking at me, but he knew my answer.

"We are going to lose the house. I can't work at that stupid company with my mother looking over my shoulder, waiting for me to make a mistake. If we have a baby, she'll let us stay. Otherwise, she's selling it out from under us."

"No," I managed to say.

Charlie stood. "No? What do you mean, no? When I met you, you said you wanted a big family, lots of kids, and a dog. The doctor said there is nothing wrong with you. You can have another baby. Isn't that why you went through labor instead of having that thing done to you."

"A D&C."

"Whatever." Charlie came into the kitchen, trapping me in a corner created by the refrigerator and the cabinets.

"It's bad enough we lost the baby. Now we're going to lose this house. Well, I'm not going to let that happen," he sneered, opening the refrigerator to look for a beer that wasn't there.

"Look. I know you haven't had your period yet, but as soon as you do, we're going to try again. If I can tell mother you're pregnant, she'll cut us some slack. And once we know it's a boy, we'll be back in her good graces."

"No. It's too soon."

"That's what you said before. And we waited, for all the good it did. You still lost the baby. This time will be different. As soon as you have your period, we'll start trying and we'll keep trying until you're pregnant."

"No," I said barely above a whisper.

"What?"

Then more loudly, "I'm not ready. I wasn't ready last time either and look what happened."

That look. I hadn't seen that look before and it scared me. I tried to slide around him, but he slammed the refrigerator door shut and stood in front of me.

"You're saying this was my fault? I rushed you into a second pregnancy before you were ready?"

We both knew it was true. I wanted to say you raped me, but I knew better. It would be like striking a match in a room filled with gasoline.

Instead, I said, "The doctor said it was no one's fault. These things can happen. Second-trimester miscarriages are rare, but they do happen."

"Rare? Rare? Well, it can't be that rare since it happened to *you* and now my life is fucked."

That was it. He was blaming me, and I wasn't going to take it.

"Your life is fucked? Really? You're not the one who went through hell delivering a dead baby. You bailed. Now you're going to lose your job because all you do is surf, not because we lost the baby, because you …" I said pointing an accusing finger at his chest, "are irresponsible and can't handle doing anything other than surf! I don't want to have a baby with you. Babies are a lot of work. Your life changes. How much help will you be? Are you still going to surf every morning and every evening leaving me to take care of everything? You need to grow up, Charlie. Grow up!"

The words "grow up" triggered something inside of him. I saw him transform from my husband to a man filled with hatred and rage. His eyes went dark, and his mouth opened to expel a cry of anguish. In two steps, he was in front of me, his hands reaching to encircle my throat, lifting me off my feet and shaking me as he screamed, "You're just like my mother, you fucking bitch. Just like my mother."

I clawed his hands and kicked his legs. What little strength I had slipped away, and blackness engulfed me.

Chapter Seventeen

High-Pitch Barking – Danger

I gasp, inhaling a shallow breath. My body is rigid as if I'm made of stone. If I could talk, I'd be speechless. I look at Charlie and I'm transported back in time. He looks the same as the first day I met him, without the multiple casts, of course—the same sun-bleached shoulder-length hair, same golden tan, same sparkling blue eyes, same winning smile. He's wearing board shorts, a white Quiksilver t-shirt, and flip-flops as if he's just come home from surfing. For an instant, I forget what he has done, but then he takes a step closer, and I remember. I retreat and slam the door. Rae is standing behind me growling, low and with menace, a sound I've only heard once before … at the parade.

It's the watcher. The man with the fake face. The man who kills squirrels with his car. The man that makes my girl afraid. I do not like this man. There is something wrong with him. I can smell it.

"Come on, Lizzy. I just want to talk. I'm better. Really, I am. Just talk to me."

His pleading voice takes me back. When I came to, in my kitchen, paramedics all around, I remember Charlie sobbing, and saying over and over again, "I'm sorry, Lizzy. So sorry." Then in the courtroom, on the day of his sentencing, as they are leading him away, he implored me with the same pleading cries.

"Lizzy. I'm sorry. I didn't mean to hurt you. I promise I'll get better, so we can be together forever."

Forever … hearing his voice again causes goosebumps to spread across my arms and the hair on the back of my neck to bristle.

Snap out of it, girl, I whisper, giving myself a mental slap in the face, before locking the door and securing the deadbolt. Moving to the dining room table, I grab a yellow pad and marker. My hands are shaking from the rush of adrenaline, so I inhale deeply to calm myself before returning to the door where Charlie is still talking, and Rae is growling, low and deep.

"I need to talk to you. I've done my time for what I did and now I'm better. Talk to me, Lizzy. Say something."

That's rich, I think.

I write—using a black marker, bold strokes and in all caps—"I CAN'T SPEAK." I tear the sheet off, fold it and push it through the mail slot. Charlie stops talking. In the silence, Rae's growl is amplified.

"Wait. You still can't speak? I thought that was a temporary thing."

I'm already writing my reply. "YOU TOOK AWAY MY VOICE. I CAN'T TALK. EVEN IF I COULD, I DON'T WANT TO TALK TO YOU. GO AWAY!" I push the paper through the slot and wait. I hope he understands that writing in all caps is the equivalent of shouting because boy, do I want to shout at him.

"I had no idea. I'm so sorry, Babe. I really am. That totally wasn't me."

When he calls me babe, a chill runs down my back that has me pulling my robe around me tighter. It does nothing to stop the chill.

"IT SURE LOOKED LIKE YOU WITH YOUR HANDS AROUND MY THROAT. NOW GO AWAY OR I'M CALLING THE POLICE." I'm so angry, I wad this message into a ball. I wish I could throw it at his face but instead, I stuff it through the slot.

There's a moment of silence as Charlie reads my message.

"Don't be like that. I'm not doing anything wrong. Let's just talk it over. I wrote you once a week, every week, while I was in that stupid hospital. Didn't your mom pass along my letters? I asked her to. I have so much I want to tell you. I'm better. I really am." He knocks on the door three times. "Let me in or come outside."

Rae loses her mind.

Danger. Danger. Bark! Bark! Bark! Bark! Bark! Bark! My girl doesn't stomp and clap. I keep barking. I will not stop until the watcher is gone.

"Geez. Can't you do something about the dog?" he asks, annoyance shading his words.

That tone is something I remember clearly. I write one more note, and slide it through the slot, before walking into the bedroom to retrieve my phone. While I'm back there, I make sure the sliding glass door is locked and the stick is in the track. I can hear Charlie talking—more like shouting—from back here in the bedroom. I step into a pair of shorts, discard the towel on my head before pulling on a t-shirt and rushing into the kitchen to check the back door. Rae continues to bark. Charlie must still be at the door.

I text 911. An operator replies, "911. What is your emergency?"

While I am texting the operator my address and asking her to send the police, Rae's bark explodes into a feverish pitch as Charlie bangs on the door again.

"Listen. I'm not going away. I know where you live now. We are meant to be together. I want to make this right. You'll see. We can start again."

Suddenly, Rae's bark shifts to a howl, her head tilted back, nose to the ceiling. A few moments later, I hear it, too, a siren off in the distance.

"God damn it, Lizzy."

The sound of the flap lifting on the mail slot brings me

back to the front door in time to watch as a red envelope slides through the opening and falls to the floor. Rae jumps back as if a firecracker has exploded. I recognize my mother's handwriting and have the answer to the question that's been bouncing around in my head ... how did he find me?

By the time the police arrive—lights flashing, siren wailing—Charlie is nowhere to be found. He is replaced by a confused UPS man who was trying to deliver a package. With Charlie gone, the only thing the police could do was file a trespassing report. Other than a physical description, I had nothing to give them ... no car description, no license plate number ... nothing. They told me to keep my doors and windows locked and not to answer the door without knowing who was on the other side. The way the house is configured, that's impossible. The porch is not flush with the front of the house but is set back five feet.

I vacillate between calling Frank or Luca, deciding Frank is the better choice. While Luca already knows about Charlie and what happened to me, I didn't want to sully my budding relationship with him with the harsh realities of my past. And besides, nothing has happened. Charlie didn't knock the door down. He didn't attack me. But still ... he did steal mail from my mother's mailbox, then drove up to Pine City to find me. Warning lights are exploding like fireworks in my head.

"You know," Frank says as he examines the sliding glass bedroom door, Rae sitting expectantly at his feet, "You two can stay with us until they find him."

Shaking my head, I text, "The odds of them finding Charlie are pretty slim. They have nothing to go on. Besides, how hard are they going to look? All he did was bang on the door. I'm not sure if that qualifies as trespassing. They are going to file a report and that will be the end of it. I can't stay at your house forever."

Frank reads my text. "Well, what about your new guy, what's his name?"

"Luca," I mouth, but he doesn't understand so I text him.

"That's it, Luca. Why don't you stay with him? I'm sure he wouldn't mind," he says with a knowing smile that has me punching him lightly on the shoulder.

Frank reaches into his pocket for a piece of beef jerky. Rae knows the drill and lies down before she's asked, then sits up, barks, and lifts her paw.

Treats. I'll lie down. I'll sit. I'll bark. I'll shake. This is the man with the treats. I like him. My girl likes him. She is calm. Not like the watcher. She does not like the watcher. This man gives me a big treat. I run to the couch to eat it.

"Too early in the relationship," I text, then follow him out of the bedroom to the kitchen.

"This is your weakest point … the window in the back door. All he has to do is break the glass, reach in, and turn the deadbolt. I can install a sliding bolt here," he says, pointing to the bottom of the door. "He wouldn't be able to reach it. If the floor is a concrete slab, I'll need my concrete drill bits. Let's take a look at the front door. We should install a peephole. You have a wooden door so it shouldn't be a problem. I know the owner. I'll call him and explain what I want to do. I'm sure he'll give me the go-ahead, especially if I don't ask him to pay for anything."

Frank has put on his "Dad hat" and is in full problem-solving mode. It makes me feel warm and fuzzy. He wasn't around when I was younger, so this is his chance to do Dad stuff. As he talks, I feel myself calming down. With Frank's fixes, I should be safer. I won't be able to leave the windows open at night, so I'll need a fan.

"Hopefully, I can get permission right away and have all this installed tomorrow, Friday at the latest."

Great, I mouth, before reverting to text. "I'm going to the garden to water. The next few days are supposed to be scorchers. Are you heading there as well?"

Frank nods. "I was there when you called. I left my hose out, and the shed open to rush right over. I'm sure I'm going to hear about it from the garden steward. I hear she's a stickler for the rules."

This makes me smile. New text … "Can I leave the dog at the garden with you for about thirty minutes? Since I can't leave the windows open tonight, I need to buy a couple of fans."

Frank looks down at Rae sitting at his feet. She lifts a paw and touches his leg. "Sure. As long as I have enough beef jerky, the two of us should be fine."

My phone pings with a new text. It's Luca.

I read his text: "Many words come to mind when thinking

about last night. None of them are adequate. See you tonight at class. I will do my best not to kiss you in front of everyone."

The man of few words has found his voice. Good sex can do that for a person.

"Are you okay?" Frank asks, mistaking my blush for something more foreboding.

I give him a thumbs up.

As soon as I'm with Luca, I know I need to tell him, but it will have to wait until after class. I channel my pent-up anger at Charlie into my lessons and the other women take notice.

Abby leans in and whispers, "What's up with you, today?" as we wait our turn to practice escaping from a grab around the waist.

I shake my head and mouth, not now.

Only two more classes after tonight before we graduate. Luca has brought in some guys from the morning classes to "attack" us and I take great pleasure in escaping from their grips.

When I disengage from a waist hold by a tall blond named Jerry, taking him to the ground then popping up into my stance ready to knock him down again, he's impressed.

"You're full of fire," Jerry says with a smile. "Let's try it again?"

Now it's my turn to smile. I give him the classic bring-it-on hand gesture before turning my back to him. This time, however, when he wraps his arms around me in a rear bear hug, he pins my arms at my sides. He's squeezing me tightly. I can't break my arms free, but I can take him down.

Spreading my legs and dropping into a squat, I swing my left leg out and behind Jerry's legs. I lean back into him, causing us both to fall backward as he trips over my outstretched leg in what is called a Valley Drop or Sacrifice Throw. The shock of hitting the ground loosens his grip allowing me to roll off, pop into my stance, and be ready if he comes at me again. I've earned a round of applause from the women, a nod from Luca, a bark from Rae, and a "Not bad," from Jerry.

Abby laughs. "Not bad? Remind me not to surprise you with a hug from behind."

"Me, too," says Sylvia.

Frank must have told Sylvia about Charlie because she adds, "You are ready for anyone who tries to mess with you ... and I do mean anyone."

Making the sign for "thank you" I return to the line.

After class, I bring Luca up to speed on what has happened.

"I should spend the night, at least until Frank makes those security changes."

I cock my head and look up at him. I wave him closer so I can whisper in his ear, "A clever ploy to get in my bed?"

"You found me out. Seriously, though, I don't think it's a bad idea. If my car is in your driveway he'll think twice about knocking on your door."

That is probably true. But Luca can't stay at my house forever and Charlie is not going to quit until he gets what he wants. I agree he can spend the night until Frank installs the peephole and sliding bolt. I remind Luca that I've been trained by a pro and am ready.

Luca shakes his head. "After watching you drop Jerry today, I almost feel sorry for the guy. Almost. He has no idea what he'll be getting himself into." Then leaning in he whispers, "If he does attack, don't hold back."

I whisper back, "I won't."

"Even if it means hurting him."

I nod.

"That's my girl," he says before lowering his lips to mine and kissing me with a desperation born of worry and concern.

Back at my house with Luca, and two four-legged alarms, I feel confident enough to open the front windows and the sliding glass door to encourage cooler air to move through the living room. I have one fan aimed at the couch where we are watching a movie and the other fan moving the warm air around in the bedroom. Both dogs are lying in front of the fan, Rae's long fur dancing around her face in the artificial breeze. It's supposed to cool to sixty-eight at some point, but right now it's still in the upper seventies and it's nine at night. We start another movie because it's still too hot to sleep, but end up dozing on the couch before the final credits.

For peace of mind, I reluctantly close the front windows and the sliding glass door, before checking all the locks. I leave one fan in the living room for the dogs who are wiped out by the heat. I'm mentally and physically exhausted from my roller coaster of a day. All I want to do is sleep. Luca understands and with his body pressing against mine, his arm draped over my waist protectively, I nod off immediately.

My girl sleeps next to the man she likes. I don't try to join them. It's too hot. I lay in front of the wind. It doesn't make me cool. I walk into the kitchen for water. Champ joins me. He has his own bowl but drinks from mine. I let him. I walk into the sleeping room. I can tell from their breathing they are both asleep. I return to the couch. With my front paws on the back of the couch, I stand guard. Nothing moves across the street. I want to tell my girl that the bad man is there. I don't know how. And so, I watch. The house is dark. His car is in front of the house. He is home. I'm tired. The noise from the wind thing makes it hard to hear. I take one more look. I see movement. A cloth is pushed aside. A face appears behind the clear wall. I look at him. He's looking at me. We don't move. I growl low and deep.

Chapter Eighteen

Whines – Sad/Scared

Thursday is grocery shopping day. I usually group other errands with grocery day, so I only make one trip into town per week. Today is no exception. During the cooler months, I take Rae with me but not in the summer. It's too hot to leave her in the car. Today, I'm making four stops including a trip to the dentist. I'll probably be gone for a couple of hours. When I return, I'll take her to the garden. She can play with Frank while I water again and harvest more tomatoes.

Unfortunately, because of Charlie, I can't leave the windows open. I keep the fan on, but it's going to get stuffy by noon. Luca has already left as he has an early morning class for people who work. I'm leaving early as well. First the dentist, then a stop at the printer, the post office to pick up a package, and finally the grocery store.

I wish there was a way to tell Rae I'll be right back. Based on her reaction—following me around, crying—she must think I'm leaving her forever. At the front door, I take a knee and hug her. I whisper in her good ear, "I'll be right back," but she only cries more. It breaks my heart every time.

My girl is leaving. I don't know when she will return. It makes me sad. I paw at her leg. Take me. She stands, opens the door, and leaves. I paw the door. I whine. Nothing happens. She doesn't come back. I lie down by the door to wait.

I wake up thirsty. I walk to the room with the food. I drink water but not a lot. I don't know how long my girl will be gone. I don't want to pee inside. I check my food bowl. There are a few pieces left. I'm not interested. I walk into the sleeping room and jump on the bed. My eyes close then fly open. Chattering. The squirrel is back. He's running across the top of the fence. I jump off the bed and bark. My nose is pressed against the clear wall. He stops and looks. He can hear me. I bark again. But the squirrel is smart. He knows I cannot get him. He continues along the fence and disappears.

I sigh. I do not like that squirrel. One day I will get him.

I trot into the big room and check the door. I listen for my girl's car. It's hard to hear with the wind thing blowing the air around. I jump onto the couch. I make three circles before I lie down. The warm air makes me sleepy. My eyes close. I wait for my girl.

I startle awake. I hear something but I'm not sure where the sound is coming from. Then I smell something that wasn't here before. It smells like meat. My nose twitches. Yes, meat. Barely cooked meat. Where is it? I jump off the couch. My nose leads me to the front door. There on the floor are three pieces of meat. I sniff. It is meat and something else. But mostly meat. I eat one. Then I eat the other two. I sniff the place where the papers slide through the door. The meat came from here. I sniff, looking for more meat. I stick my nose in. There is some meat here. I lick the metal edges. I listen. I don't hear anything. The wind thing is loud. The floor in front of the door is cool. I make three circles and lay down. I close my eyes.

A noise wakes me. I feel odd. My eyes don't want to open. I lift my head. It feels heavy. I hear more noises from the room with the food. What is happening? Maybe Lizzy is home. I open my eyes. I hear a voice. It is not Lizzy. I whimper. It's the watcher.

He is talking. He is using a calm voice. He is carrying something. He walks to me slowly like he is afraid. I growl as he comes closer. He stops. More talking. I don't know what he is saying. The calm voice, again, before stepping closer.

He is not supposed to be here. I want to bark at him. I am very tired. He comes closer. I growl and bare my teeth. Then he pounces. The thing he is holding is placed over my nose and mouth. I can breathe. I can smell. I cannot bite. I keep growling. I can tell the watcher is not afraid of me now. He picks me up. I want to struggle. I am very tired. He opens the door. He carries me across the street to the dark car. He places me in the back. I like to ride in the front with Lizzy. Lizzy is not here. I am sad. I whine and whine. The watcher says something. This time he does not use a calm voice. He sounds angry. I curl up. I close my eyes. As the car begins to move, I fall asleep.

I am being carried again by the watcher. To a new place. I sniff. The trees that smell like sugar are here. I open my eyes. There are many, many tall trees. Their scent is strong. The man is holding me tight. I do not wiggle. He walks up the stairs to a wooden house. He places me on the ground. I want to run away. My legs are not working. I lie down. I hear jangling metal. He opens the door. He picks me up, saying something I don't understand.

This man talks and talks. He doesn't know the signs Lizzy uses. He places me on a couch. It smells dusty and stale. It is dark in here. The man does not turn on a light. There is a cloth covering a glass wall. The man does not move the cloth away. It blocks the sun. The man does not give me water. I use my paws. The cage on my face does not move. I whine. I make a small bark. The man says something. His voice is harsh. I stay quiet. The man takes off the collar around my neck. Then the man leaves. He closes the door. Then the jangle of metal and a click. The car starts. There is a sound of crunching rocks. Then there is silence. I whine. No one is here. I am too tired to look around. I close my eyes and sleep.

It's been almost three hours since I left Rae. She's fine, but I still feel bad about leaving her for so long. I'm looking forward to a joyful reunion with much tail wagging and yips of happiness. I've turned off the engine and am opening my door when movement on the street catches my eye. The neighbor across the street is backing out of the driveway. Walking to the tailgate to retrieve my groceries, I watch as the Jeep parks itself across my driveway. The windows have a deep tint so it's not until the door opens that I see him.

This time, there will be no hesitation. The fact that he purposefully blocked my car is proof enough that his intentions are not friendly. I face him, ready. In my mind, I go through different defensive moves. What do I do if he grabs my arm? What do I do if he grabs me with two hands or if he goes for my throat, wraps me in a bear hug and tries to carry me away? I almost hope he tries it … almost. Then he says the one thing for which I have no defense.

"I have your dog."

He tosses me her collar, which I catch. I am stunned. Not Rae. With four simple words, Charlie pulled the plug on my fight or flight adrenaline, which swirls away like water down a drain. Fear and anger mix in the pit of my stomach. Without thinking, I rush him and before he can react, I use my fists to pound his chest with all my strength, fueled by rage. I manage to deliver several hits before he grabs my wrists and stops me. The moment his hands wrap around my wrists, my training kicks in and I free myself, stepping back out of his reach.

"Jesus, Lizzy," he says, rubbing his chest.

It's a good thing I can't speak, or I'd be screaming at him, "You better not have hurt her."

As if he can read my mind, he says, "Your dog is fine. I'm not a monster."

You strangled your wife. You kidnapped my dog. I beg to differ.

"I'll take you to her."

Looking across the street, I realize he's been here all along … watching my every move. I take several steps, moving to cross the street.

"Stop. She's not there. I'm not an idiot. She's at a cabin in the woods. Very secluded and quiet. We'll be able to talk. Get in the Jeep."

That means there won't be any neighbors I can run to for help. I move to retrieve my pack.

"Leave it. Get in."

He opens the passenger door. What choice do I have? He has found my Achilles heel and her name is Rae.

Arms crossed under my chest I stare ahead as Charlie drives. I pay attention to where we are going … west on the main boulevard through town, past where the high school band marched in the parade, past the last business, past the last housing tract. Then we take a left and head up a winding road. I make a mental note of the street name, "Cedar Falls Road." About a mile later, the paved road ends and turns to dirt. I've never spent much time at this end of the valley, but it will be fairly easy to find my way back … follow the road downhill.

Charlie is chattering away as if we are off on an exciting adventure instead of the hostage situation it feels like to me. He's going on about how he's enjoyed his time in the mountains these last few weeks, but the beach is still his thing. I try to remember the first time the black Jeep was parked in the driveway across the street. Three, maybe four weeks ago. I also remember how Rae did not like the Jeep when we did our sniff about. She knew something I didn't. If only dogs could talk. Now Charlie is asking me if I knew that he'd been allowed to surf while in the hospital. When I learned the hospital was in Malibu, the thought did cross my mind. Sounds like this hospital of his was a minimum-security summer camp for "loonies" as my mother called them.

"You would have known about the surfing and the other stuff if you had bothered to read my letters," he says, shifting into 4-wheel drive as the road grows steeper. "It hurt my feelings that you never wrote back. It was nice of your mom to send me cards, though. At least someone cared."

Did mom send him cards? She never told me that. When I asked her to throw Charlie's letters away, she'd protested. "Are you sure? Maybe he's sorry. Maybe he's changed. I can't believe you want me to throw them away."

Finally, she agreed. I thought that was the end of it. Then, after about six months, she let slip something Charlie had said in a letter, so she had to admit she was reading them. I'd been so angry at her. I'd stopped texting and answering her calls for a week. She defended her actions by saying she was only trying to protect me. By reading Charlie's letters, she could stay "in the know," learn what he was up to and collect information about his release date. But sending Charlie cards ... that was just too much. I'll confront her later. Right now, I need to concentrate on how to get away once I have Rae.

A few more bumpy yards and we turn left again, climbing up an even steeper road, which turns out not to be a road but a long, dirt driveway. Near the top, there's a small log cabin surrounded by trees. The tires crunch on a flat gravel parking area as we slow to a stop. I've been paying attention and am confident that I can find my way back to the main highway from here. Now I have to figure out how to escape with Rae. I follow Charlie up the steps. If Rae is here, she should be barking by now. She would have heard the car and the key in the door. I follow Charlie inside, but Rae doesn't run to me.

It's a small Forest Service cabin, which means people don't stay year-round. I take in the layout ... open floor plan with a slab of wood acting as a breakfast bar separating the small kitchen from the living room. A staircase leads to a second-floor loft. In the dim light, I can make out old furniture, a stone fireplace, and two closed doors along the back wall, which I assume leads to a bedroom or a bathroom.

I want to scream, "Where is she?" when I hear a soft

thumping. There, lying on a worn-out sofa, is my baby, her tail beating against the couch. I rush over as Charlie turns on the lights. Rae is wearing a muzzle and whining. The first thing I do is release the straps at the back of her head. She makes a small yip and then licks my hand. She licks, and licks, and licks. Her tail never stops thumping.

My girl. My girl is here. I want to jump all over her. I am still tired. It is easier now to keep my eyes open. I look up. Water leaks from her eyes and drips off her face. I want to lick her. I lift my head. Her face is far away. I lick her hand. I am happy now. We are together. I am thirsty. I hope my girl will bring me water. My mouth is dry. The watcher is here. He is staying away. That is good. The cage is off my face. If he comes close, I will bite him.

I'm so relieved that she is safe. I pull her into my arms. She is as limp as a wet washcloth. I turn and look at Charlie who is keeping his distance. I mouth the words, "What the hell?" very slowly so there is no mistaking my question.

"Relax, babe. She's fine."

I pantomime a cup of water. If Rae has been here since this morning with that muzzle, she is probably thirsty. He acts like he doesn't know what I want.

Charlie picks up a yellow pad and throws it at me like a frisbee. It lands at my feet with a thud. Then he throws a marker pen, end-over-end, which lands on the couch.

"So, you can talk."

Grabbing the pad and marker I write, "Bring me a bowl of

water for my dog."

"Say please."

I want to flip him off but instead, I write, "Please."

"There. Was that so difficult?"

You have no idea. I watch him look in the cupboards for a bowl.

He delivers the water before walking to an overstuffed chair directly across from the couch. He tosses a decorative pillow on the floor and makes himself comfortable.

I hold the bowl so Rae can drink. Her pink tongue laps at the water until there is nothing left. My poor baby. I'm so sorry this has happened to you. But I'm here now. When I leave, we will leave together. I promise.

"Ready to talk?" Charlie asks, leaning back in his chair, a smile on his face.

I place the empty bowl on the floor and retrieve the pad and pen. I write, "FUCK YOU!" then tear the sheet off, crumple it into a ball, and throw it at his face. It is a highly ineffective form of aggression but boy, does it feel good. He catches the paper ball easily, peels it open, reads, then looks up, the smile never leaving his lips.

"Nice."

Chapter Nineteen

Tail Thump – Happy

Since we arrived, Charlie has been talking like a river flowing down a mountain … fast, noisy, and with tremendous energy.

"I'm sorry it has to be this way, babe, but you gave me no choice. You didn't answer my letters and you wouldn't talk to me willingly, so here we are."

I write, "What do you want?"

"I want to get back together. Start over. Be a family, again."

"Not going to happen." I show him what I've written, and he shakes his head.

"I'm here to change your mind."

"You think kidnapping my dog will change my mind?

What did you give her? When will she snap out of it?" I ask, holding up the pad.

"It's a sedative. Trazodone … very effective. It's amazing what you can find online. I didn't even need a vet. I just ordered it and two days later it arrived at the cabin. Your dog will be fine in about four to five hours."

Four to five hours from now. or four to five hours from when she took the pill? I'm hoping it's from when she took the pill, which would mean she will snap out of it sooner than later. There is no way I can escape if I have to carry forty pounds of dead weight. I'd be vulnerable and couldn't defend myself. Either I have to stay until Rae can walk or figure out something else. I could take Charlie's Jeep, but I had watched as he stuffed the keys deep in his front pocket. I can't think of a way to get the keys. I wish I had learned offensive moves as well as defense in my Jiu-Jitsu class. A good knockout punch or kick would do the trick.

Charlie interrupts my thoughts. "Let's start at the beginning. First off, I need to say I'm sorry for what I did. If you'd bothered to read my letters, then you'd know how sorry I am. I'm not an abusive person, you know that. It's not who I am. It's just that sometimes, I get so frustrated and angry that I can't control my emotions. At the hospital, they had a name for it, intermittent explosive disorder. I won't bore you with all the details, but after months of therapy and medication, I'm fine now."

While Charlie is talking, I stroke Rae from head to tail. She thumps her tail. I need to come up with a plan.

"Here's another thing I found out. When I attacked you, it wasn't you I was attacking."

I stop petting Rae long enough to write, "Oh really? Because I could have sworn it was your hands around my throat."

By the look on his face, I can tell he's picked up on my sarcasm.

"Of course, it was you, but it wasn't. You told me to 'grow up.' That's the same thing my mother has said to me all my life. When Phillip died I cried on and off for weeks. She couldn't handle my crying. She thought I should hold my feelings in like a man … like she did. She told me to grow up. Men don't fall apart. Men carry on. Be a man. Grow up. Those were the messages I received every day until I stopped crying. She'd say, 'You're the oldest now. Stop 'screwing around with surfing and take on the family responsibilities.' Two hours before our fight, she'd called, urging me to get back on the horse—"

I write one word, "horse?" Then wad it up and throw it at him. Rae moans with the movement.

After reading my comment he says, "Come on. It's a phrase. She wasn't calling you a horse."

I'm guessing that's exactly what she was doing, but I let it go.

Charlie shakes his head. I watch him take a deep breath and exhale slowly. "As I was saying, babe, she was telling us that we should try again, explaining how important it was that we have a baby to carry on the family business. I tried to tell her about the surf school, but she shut that down. I explained that we had plenty of time to have a baby. What's the rush? Then, and I quote, 'Even if you do decide to run the family business, we both know you lack the skill, tenacity, and desire to be an effective leader. You are simply a placeholder until your son can take the reins.'"

Catherine is the one who needs a therapist.

"I pushed back. Told her she was a bitch. She laughed. Then she said, "Grow up." I was so angry, I hung up on her. Then, a day later, you say the same thing. It triggered the anger I felt toward my mother, and I lost it. According to my therapist, when I was strangling you, I was symbolically strangling my mother."

What he was saying may or may not be true, but I was the one who almost died, not his mother. And I am the one who lost her voice, not his mother. I feel sorry for him. I do. But that doesn't mean we're getting back together ... ever. When he almost killed me, he killed any feelings I had for him as well.

"I've learned so much. I meditate every morning. I take my drugs. I have breathing techniques I use if I feel anxious. I'm a new person. And this new person is ready to bring our family back together."

I write. "I divorced you. I have a new life. I've moved on and so should you." Tear, wad, throw.

"Can you stop doing that?" he asks as he catches the paper ball.

What? I mouth with a slight shrug.

"Just show me what you've written. You don't have to

throw it at me."

Write … "But I like it. It's MY coping mechanism. It's *my* therapy." Tear, wad, throw.

"Fine. Look. I didn't come all this way for you to say no without fully understanding what I've been through, how I've changed, and what our future could be. I understand how much my mother interfered in our lives. But that's over. I've severed all ties … new phone number, new apartment, new financial strings. We can move. Find a place just for us. She won't know where we live."

I shake my head.

"I know we are technically divorced. But that can be fixed. And by the way, I thought it was pretty shitty … divorcing me while I was in a hospital."

A mental institution, not a hospital, on a beach in Malibu where they let you surf. I feel no sympathy.

"But I get it and I forgive you."

Well, good for you. Maybe you should ask if I've forgiven you, which I haven't.

"I have it all figured out. We can get married again and this time plan everything … on the beach, in real sand, whatever you want. Then you and I can choose a house together. We probably can't afford a house like the one my parents bought but maybe one that's close enough to the beach so it's not a long drive to the waves. Whatever you want."

He keeps saying "whatever you want" but all I've heard is

what he wants. What I want is to stay in the mountains and for Charlie to leave me alone. But of course, even now, this isn't about me.

"I still have a trust fund, so I have money. Not as much as I would if I worked for The Company, but I'm not doing that. I had a long time to think while I was locked up. So much time."

And then, as if he's finally remembered that I would be part of this equation he adds, "And you can do whatever ... go back to work, stay at home. I want you to be happy, too. No pressure to have kids."

Thank you for giving me permission to do what I want.

"We can just have a dog, no kids if that's what you want."

I write, "I already have a dog. The dog you drugged and kidnapped." Tear, wad, and toss with added force.

"The dog is fine. I only gave her one pill."

My eyes narrow into slits. I wish I could shoot laser beams from my angry eyes. The look on his face tells me he's received my message loud and clear.

"Come on, Babe. She'll be fine." Charlie stands and walks my way as if he plans on sitting on the couch. I put my hand out like a stop sign and shake my head. Then I point to his chair.

Charlie does stop but he doesn't sit down. "Thirsty?"

I am, so I nod. He heads into the kitchen, and I follow him with my eyes. He sets his phone on a bar that divides the kitchen from the living room. If I take his phone, and disappear into the bathroom, I can call the police.

"Water, soda, or beer?"

It's like he expects me to shout out an answer. Instead, I write, "soda," then hold up the pad so he can see it.

Charlie smiles. "That wasn't so hard, was it?"

So condescending. I want to slap that smile off his face. He returns, handing me a can of off-brand cola before returning to his chair. The stuff tastes terrible, but I drink it, thinking this will give credence to my claim that I have to pee. I'll just need to listen to him for a while longer.

He's back in his chair now, settling into the story of his hospital stay. His first therapist was a clueless twit, but his second doctor was okay. (She listened and made him feel heard.) The other patients were all worse off than he was, of course. (He calls them the crazies, which makes me want to laugh. My mother would have said, "I told you they were all loonies.") His room was smaller than any place he's ever lived. (He felt claustrophobic and had trouble sleeping.) But surfing saved his sanity. (The break was lame, but it was better than working in a stupid vegetable garden.) And the food … the food was passable, but nothing compared to my cooking. (His favorite days were Taco Tuesday and Sushi Friday.) Surfing and sushi … what an ordeal. During this entire dramatic monologue, he never asks about me, or how I'd been surviving without being able to speak. It's all about Charlie. Thinking back, it always was.

Rae is still not moving even though I am scratching behind her ears. While I'm half listening to Charlie drone on—nodding and smiling—I'm formulating a plan. It starts with asking for something to eat.

"I'm hungry. Do you have anything?" I write. This time I don't throw the message at him. Let him think I'm coming around.

Charlie perks up. A smile lit up his face because now I'm being reasonable. "I do."

When he stands, I lift Rae's head off my thigh and slide out from under her. She whines in her sleep. My poor little girl. Taking the pad and the marker with me, I follow Charlie to the kitchen. I stand on the living room side of the counter while Charlie opens the refrigerator.

Looking around the door he says, "I have tuna but forgot the mayo, or I have bologna and mustard."

Fine dining for sure. I write bologna in large letters and show him the pad. Then I set the pad on the counter covering his cell phone, hoping he doesn't notice. He doesn't. He's too busy talking. I watch as he lays out six slices of white bread on the counter like he's dealing poker and then slaps a slice of bologna on each piece followed by decorative swirls of mustard. He makes a happy face on one. I haven't had a bologna sandwich since I was a kid. It makes me think of Charlie as a scared little boy … hiding from his mother, only capable of making cheap bologna sandwiches cut into triangles because that's what you do when you are mentally a ten-year-old. He opens cabinets until he finds plates.

With two triangles on my plate and four on his, he asks, "Do you want to eat here or back on the couch?"

I motion with a tilt of my head to return to the living room. As I retrieve my pad of paper, I make sure I have a hold of his phone as well. Back on the couch, I place the notepad on my lap, letting the phone fall between my legs. I leave the pad in place to use as a table. Charlie hands me my plate and I set it on the pad. So far, so good.

"Oh. I forgot. I have chips."

As he returns to the kitchen, my body tenses waiting for him to discover his missing phone. Thankfully, he doesn't notice and returns with a bag of barbeque potato chips. He offers me the open bag and I reach inside for a handful. Feeling emboldened by his lack of awareness, I pantomime that I'd like another drink. While I don't plan on drinking this one, I use the opportunity to move the phone from between my legs to my back pocket while he is behind the open refrigerator door.

I eat in silence, like I have a choice, while Charlie talks with his mouth full.

"Remember my surfing school idea?"

He doesn't wait for me to nod. He's talking faster and faster, now.

"I have a couple of surfing bros who are all in as instructors. We're thinking of either Huntington Beach or Malibu. And the best part, we wouldn't need an office. Everything will be online, except for the actual classes, of course. We'll buy a toy hauler, you know, the trailers that have a garage in the rear? It will double as an office and surfboard storage. It even has a bathroom.

It's perfect, right?"

Giving him a reassuring smile, I nod. He's almost done eating. That's when I'll make my move.

"There's this guy who can paint a sick design on both sides. It'll become a rolling billboard when we drive to and from the beach. I spent a ton of time at the hospital drawing different scenes for the trailer. I even created a logo. The art instructor said I have natural talent," he says, smiling with pride.

Art classes, surfing, sushi Fridays … I want to go to this mental hospital.

"The logo needs some work, but a professional will be able to clean it up. I can show it to you. I have pictures on my phone of my rough drafts."

Oh, no. Tension ripples through my body as he looks around. Managing my breathing, I'm ready for him to accuse me, and he does.

"Have you seen my phone?"

I shake my head, then pick up my pad and write, "Maybe you left it in the car."

Then, needing to act now, I write, "Which door is the bathroom? All this soda …"

Charlie points to a door near the staircase. "I'm going to check the Jeep." Then as an afterthought, he says, the previous friendliness replaced by a thinly veiled menace, "The front door is the only way out and there isn't a window in the bathroom, just in case you were thinking of trying something."

Shaking my head, I point to my sleeping dog.

"Oh, right. You'd never leave without your precious pup." He makes "precious" sound like a dirty word.

I stand and wait for him to walk to the front door before I can turn around. I can't let him see the outline of his phone in my back pocket. He hesitates as if he knows I'm up to something, so I stall by bending to pet Rae, scratch behind her ears, and rub her back. Charlie lets out a disgusted sigh as I fawn over my dog. Finally, he turns for the door.

Now's my chance. I rush to the bathroom, close and lock the door, before silencing the ringer and turning the volume down. Pressing the side button and the volume simultaneously, I'm rewarded with an emergency SOS slide. I swipe to the right at the precise moment Charlie bangs on the door. I flinch so violently that I bobble the phone, catching it before it hits the floor.

"What are you doing in there?"

I wish I could say, "What do you think?" Instead, I flush the toilet and turn on the water. As the water is running, I look around for a place to hide his phone. I'm hoping the SOS will alert the police and they will be able to follow the GPS signal to this location. I open a cupboard to find extra bath towels and slide the phone between two towels before closing the door quietly. I run my hands under the water and wipe them on my shorts.

"Open up," Charlie says, banging again.

I unlock the door and Charlie pushes his way into the bathroom. "I can't find my phone. I remember bringing it inside.

You took it, didn't you?"

I do my best to look innocent, shrug my shoulders, make a face, shake my head. I don't think he's buying it. He spins me around and pats my back pockets. He glances around the bathroom. Not finding his phone, he pushes past me again, swearing. I follow him out. Charlie searches around the cushions of the old chair.

"God damn it."

He looks over his shoulder and cuts his eyes at me. He knows I've done something, but he can't figure out what. I return to the couch and put a protective arm around Rae. That's when I feel it. A growl is rumbling deep inside of her. I hope this means she's coming out of it. I'm not sure if the police will be able to home in on this exact house or just the general area. We are in the mountains with pockets of dead zones, but his phone had three bars, so I'm hopeful.

Charlie is pacing now. I need to calm him down.

"I'm sure it will turn up," I write.

Charlie drops into the chair, arms folded across his chest, staring at me. "You took my phone. I know you did. I'm not sure what good that did."

"I did nothing. Why are you so paranoid?" I show him the pad.

"I'm not paranoid. I just don't trust you. If you think you're in charge here, you are mistaken."

Maybe the old Lizzy was helpless against you, but this

Lizzy is not. My biggest challenge is Rae, otherwise, I would walk out of here, daring him to stop me. I scratch behind Rae's ears more vigorously. Then I dig my fingers into her fur and give her backside a good jostling hoping to rouse her. She thumps her tail. Yes. She's responding.

"You sure do love that stupid dog," Charlie says, watching me bend down so I can whisper in her ear.

He isn't wrong, except for the stupid part. I would pretty much do anything for my fur baby including willingly climbing into a car with my crazy ex. Rae lifts her head and licks my nose.

"Disgusting."

Charlie stands and walks into the kitchen where he pulls a beer out of the refrigerator. Good. Maybe it will relax him.

When he returns to his chair, he asks, "Where were we?"

I remember what we were talking about—his surfing business—but I don't want to bring it up, reminding him about his phone. Instead, I write, "When are you going to let us go home?"

"Home? Do you mean that house where I found you? That's not your home. Your home is with me. We're married. I didn't sign any divorce papers."

I don't have enough paper or the patience to explain how I didn't need his permission or signature since he was in a mental hospital!

I write, "I'm supposed to have dinner with my father tonight." It's a lie, but he won't know that. I continue. "He will wonder where I am when I don't show up. When he finds my car with the groceries inside, he will call the police."

"Your father? Really? Where was this father when we got married? You told me you didn't know your father. Not buying it," he says with a smirk. "Maybe that boyfriend of yours will come sniffing around with his dog, but probably not today since you would have said that instead of making up a story about an imaginary father."

Charlie is acting like he's Sherlock Holmes and he's very proud of his deductive reasoning. I don't argue with him. I want him to keep talking. How long has it been since I activated the SOS? Is someone coming and will they be able to find me? If nothing happens in the next fifteen minutes, I'll need to go to plan B, whatever that is.

Charlie continues. "Even if the boyfriend shows up, there is no way he'll know where you are. Besides, we're not staying here for long. As soon as it's dark, we're driving off this mountain," he says with a sly smile that sets my mind spinning.

Rae lifts her head, her ears coming to attention. She makes a low howl deep in her throat. This is it.

"What's up with her?"

I write, "She has to pee." I show Charlie then stand.

Rae sits up and looks around. Again, with another howl, this one louder. I slap my thigh, my signal for her to come. Not with her ordinary grace, Rae does her best to leave the couch, first her front paws, then her back. She's following me to the door. Good. The drug is wearing off. She barks once. She probably really does have to pee. I'm almost to the front door when I hear it. A siren. Rae points her nose in the air and lets out a full-throated howl. My hand is on the doorknob.

"Oh, no you don't," Charlie roars.

I yank the door open. Rae rushes out. But before I can cross the threshold, Charlie wraps his arms around my waist and drags me back inside. I am ready.

Chapter Twenty

Howl – I Hear Something

My girl is rubbing my back. She's scratching my head. I'm feeling more awake. I thump my tail to let her know I like the rubbing. I open my eyes. I do not like this place. It smells bad. I turn my head. The watcher is here. Lizzy is tense. There is danger here. Lizzy whispers in my ear, "Good girl. Good Rae, Rae. Wake up, please."

I lift my head and lick her on the nose. The Watcher says something. His tone is mean. Then I hear it. It's far away. A high-pitched call. I howl deep inside. Does my girl hear it? I howl again.

Lizzy is standing. She is slapping her thigh. Slap, slap, slap. She wants me to come. I stand. My legs are not working right. I climb off the couch instead of jumping. I follow my girl to the door.

Now that I'm walking, I need to pee. I bark. Lizzy is going to let me outside. That sound is closer, louder. I tilt my head back and howl. Lizzy opens the door. I walk outside.

My feet are not touching the ground as Charlie pulls me back from the door. My training kicks in. I bend at the waist and reach down between my legs. I grab a hold of his leg with both hands around his calf. Then, deep breath, I push my back into him as I pull his leg up. We are falling. Charlie hits the ground with a thud as I jerk his leg in a direction it is not meant to go.

I hear two sounds … bone snapping, and Charlie's scream.

No time to feel sorry for him. I roll off, pop up and step away, out of reach. But he is not coming after me. He's curled into the fetal position, wailing in pain.

"You broke my fucking leg!"

He's lucky that's all I did, because I'm resisting the urge to kick him while he's down. Instead, I scream. It's a truly horrible sound, like a banshee howl right before it swoops in for a kill. Charlie shuts up, his eyes wide. He looks scared and he should be because, right now, I want to do him harm by taking out all my anger and rage on him. Lucky for Charlie, I'm not a violent person.

Grabbing the pad and marker, I rush to the door, a string of curses following in my wake. I find Rae lying at the bottom of the steps, a dark wet patch of dirt a few feet away. She did have to pee. A siren is growing louder. I slap my thigh. Rae reluctantly stands. I jog down the steep dirt road picking up speed, worrying that the police will drive past. Rae is walking in slow motion but at least she's moving. The siren is very close. Rae howls in answer. I'm almost to the intersection of the driveway and the road when I spot the white sheriff's vehicle. I wave the pad of paper in the air like a signal flag. They see me. I let out a huge breath I didn't realize I'd been holding as they turn up the driveway. They silence the siren as they turn up the long driveway and pull to a stop next to me.

The officer rolls down the window.

"Did you call 911?"

I nod, then use the pad and marker to explain the situation.

Thirty minutes later, the once secluded driveway is a traffic jam of vehicles—three sheriff cars including the one that brought Detective Mendoza, the female detective who conducted the interviews when Berta turned up dead, a fire truck, and an ambulance for Charlie (I recognize one of the firemen, Brian), and Frank's car. Using Charlie's phone after he reluctantly gave me his passcode—my birthday—I called Frank.

We are sitting on the edge of the porch, Frank, Rae, and me, our legs dangling over the edge, while the paramedics are inside preparing Charlie for a ride to the hospital. Frank has his arm draped protectively across my shoulder. It feels good. The adrenaline has dissipated, and I'm left feeling drained and exhausted. I lean into Frank and for the first time, I think of him as my dad. For thirty-six years, I didn't know I had a father. It's been difficult thinking of Frank that way, but not anymore.

Rae puts a paw on Frank's leg.

"Sorry, girl. I don't have any treats for you."

One of the officers climbs the steps. "Hey, Frank. Bury any bodies lately?"

I feel Frank shake his head. "Good one. Like I haven't heard that before."

Moments later, Detective Mendoza comes outside and walks down the stairs. "How are you doing?"

I give her a thumbs up.

"I've sent an officer to your house. You said your dog was locked inside, which means Mr. Bouchard must have broken in. That elevates dognapping to a felony. I'll let you know your options."

"When can she go home? Her bag, keys, phone, and groceries have been sitting in her unlocked car all day," Frank says.

"You can pick up the car now. I'll give you a call when our people are done with the house," Mendoza says.

I make the sign for "Thank you."

"You two seem to have a way of getting in trouble. I hope this is the end of it," Mendoza says with a smile.

I cross my heart.

Rae's head pops up as the paramedics maneuver Charlie out the door on a wheeled stretcher. Frank and I stand. Charlie's leg is in a splint. Ironic. The first time and hopefully the last time I've seen Charlie he's had a broken leg.

"Hold up," Frank asks before they take Charlie down the stairs.

Frank walks over to Charlie, bends in close, and whispers something in his ear. Charlie turns a paler shade of white.

Frank straightens. "We're good now. Right, Charlie?"

Charlie turns his face away. I wonder what Frank said to him.

We follow the paramedics down the stairs, Rae trailing behind. Once at the car, Frank opens the door, but before I climb in, I wrap my arms around him. Frank responds, encircling me in an embrace. When we separate, I motion for him to come closer.

I stretch up on tiptoes and whisper in his ear, "I love you, Dad."

When Frank straightens, the smile on his face is radiant. "I love you, too. Now let's get you and the Rabbit Slayer home."

I motion again for him to lean down then I whisper, "Her name is Rae."

Chapter Twenty-One
Five Months Later

Everyone is shouting. The man with the treats is acting strange. I bark at him. He laughs. I don't understand. There is no danger here. My girl is happy. She is with her man. He has his arm around her. Lizzy is safe. But why is everyone shouting? I lay my head on Lizzy's thigh. People are weird.

Dad has his hands tucked into his armpits and is flapping around like a bird.

Mom shouts, "Chicken."

Dad shakes his head. He sticks out his butt and wiggles his bottom, then walks like a duck.

"Duck," shouts Sylvia.

Dad nods, looking relieved that he can stop. He holds up three fingers, then one, and flaps like a duck.

Eric recaps. "Three words. The first word is duck."

Mom looks up at Eric like he's Einstein.

Dad nods. Then holds up two fingers.

"Second word," says Sylvia.

Frank makes the gesture for a small word, and everyone starts shouting out little words until someone says "and" and Frank touches his nose.

Frank moves on to the third word. As he goes through his pantomime, I look around the room. The living room is the epitome of Christmas coziness. There is a crackling fire, mugs of warm coffee, and family all around. My mom and her boyfriend Eric are practically sitting on top of each other like a couple of teenagers. Champ is sleeping under the Christmas tree, a ball of discarded holiday wrapping under his front paws. The dining room table still has the plates and forks left from dessert. Uncharacteristically, Sylvia said we'd deal with the dishes later. She was itching to play charades, although she teased me about having an unfair advantage. I look down at my sweet Rae. As I scratch her head, my new diamond ring catches the firelight and sparkles. I lean into Luca, who looks at me with love in his eyes and squeezes my arm.

I realize I finally have the family I wanted. Maybe not the one I imagined, but a family just the same.

Frank is on his knees cowering. Acting out pulling something over his head.

"Afraid."

"Scared."

"A baby," says Mom, which earns her a scowl from Frank.

Three words. Duck and … using my pad and pen I write, "cover" and then show it to Luca.

"Cover … Duck and Cover," Luca says loud enough to be heard over the other shouts.

"Yes!" Frank sighs, touching his finger to his nose. "Finally."

Rae pops her head up and barks. *Woof!* She always has to have the last word.

Woof!

Rae's Favorite Blueberry Dog Treats

Ingredients

1 ¾ cups uncooked oatmeal

1 large banana

½ cup peanut butter

¼ cup dried blueberries

Preheat the oven to 350 degrees. Mash the banana. Stir in the peanut butter and blueberries. Using a food processor or blender, grind the oatmeal until it resembles flour. Add 1 ½ cups of the oat flour to the banana/peanut butter mixture, stirring until blended. Sprinkle the remaining ¼ cup of oat flour onto a flat surface. Roll out the dough to ¼ inch thickness. Using a cookie cutter, cut the dough into shapes. I use a dog bone cookie cutter. Place cookies on a parchment paper lined cookie sheet and bake for 15 minutes. Cool completely before giving to your favorite pet! Store in an airtight container.

Made in the USA
Columbia, SC
26 April 2023

15575534R00148